"I'm sorry if I kept you waiting."

She was doing her damnedest not to drool. All that brawny muscle. All that masculine beauty. Was it any wonder that she'd kept sleeping with him after the divorce? "I texted you. But I didn't realize you were on the beach."

"I didn't bring my phone with me. Do you want to come in while I get dressed?"

"No, thanks. I'll stay here."

He gripped his board. "I'm not going to shower. I can do that later."

"You don't hav█████████████████████████

"I don't mind. ████████████████████████ng. The least I ca█████████████████

He entered th████████████████████████ her thoughts. Her █████████████████ body-hugging shorts. The surfer-boy smell of his skin. The affair she was missing.

Why couldn't she just lose interest in him?

* * *

Hollywood Ex Factor by Sheri WhiteFeather is part of the LA Women series.

Dear Reader,

Where were you born and how many different places have you lived? I was born in Clearfield, Pennsylvania, but my family moved to California when I was two. Since then, I've had some stopovers in Portland, Oregon. But mostly I spent my life in California. Not in one area, though. I moved a lot.

Here's a list of the places in California where I've lived: San Jose, Glendale, Los Alamitos, Cypress, Hollywood, North Hollywood, Littlerock (yes, there is a Littlerock, CA), Burbank, Orange, Anaheim, Bakersfield, Sun City and Menifee. Whew! That's a lot of places.

Can you guess my favorite? It was Hollywood. I loved that wild town. Every so often, Hollywood creeps into my books. It's making a big splash in this one.

Hollywood Ex Factor features a divorced couple still steeped in each other. Margot is a former child star/actress, and Zeke is a bodyguard/security specialist who was raised in Beverly Hills with a celebrity mom and a talent agent dad.

It doesn't get any more Hollywood than that. But there's more to Margot and Zeke than where they grew up. So much more...

Happy reading,

Sheri WhiteFeather

SHERI
WHITEFEATHER

—

HOLLYWOOD EX FACTOR

HARLEQUIN
DESIRE

Recycling programs for this product may not exist in your area.

ISBN-13: 978-1-335-23293-9

Hollywood Ex Factor

Copyright © 2021 by Sheree Henry-WhiteFeather

This edition published by arrangement with Harlequin Books S.A.

For questions and comments about the quality of this book, please contact us at CustomerService@Harlequin.com.

Harlequin Enterprises ULC
22 Adelaide St. West, 40th Floor
Toronto, Ontario M5H 4E3, Canada
www.Harlequin.com

Printed in U.S.A.

Sheri WhiteFeather is an award-winning bestselling author. She lives in Southern California and enjoys shopping in vintage stores and visiting art galleries and museums. She is known for incorporating Native American elements into her books and has two grown children who are tribally enrolled members of the Muscogee Creek Nation. Visit her website at www.sheriwhitefeather.com.

Books by Sheri WhiteFeather

Harlequin Desire

Sons of Country

Wrangling the Rich Rancher
Nashville Rebel
Nashville Secrets

Daughters of Country

Hot Nashville Nights
Wild Nashville Ways

LA Women

Hollywood Ex Factor

Visit her Author Profile page at Harlequin.com, or www.sheriwhitefeather.com, for more titles.

You can also find Sheri WhiteFeather on Facebook, along with other Harlequin Desire authors, at Facebook.com/harlequindesireauthors!

One

Frustrated by it all, Zeke Mitchell unbuckled his seat belt, preparing to exit the plane. He'd just spent four hours and fifty-one minutes in the air, obsessing about his ex.

He should be glad to be home. But instead, he was stressing over Margot Jensen. She was an actress and one of his LA clients. She was also his occasional lover. But most important, she was his former wife. They'd started sleeping together soon after their divorce, which was going on three years now. An uncommitted affair, he thought.

Sporadic, sex-only hookups.

But that might be coming to an end. Margot had texted him last night, saying that she was having second thoughts about their affair and wanted to discuss it with him.

He stood and removed his carry-on from above his seat, then disembarked with the rest of the first-class passengers and proceeded to the baggage reclaim area to collect the remainder of his luggage. From there, he headed outside to ground transportation, where he'd already arranged for a town car to take him straight to Margot's. She'd asked him to come by as soon as he could, but he was fine with that. He wanted to get their damned discussion over with.

He blew out a sigh. What did he expect? To have a fling with his ex-wife forever? At some point, their affair was meant to crash and burn. Then again, maybe he could convince her to be together one last time...

Damn it. Why did Margot have to affect him this way? Why couldn't he shake her from his blood?

He cleared his mind and scanned the cars lined up at the curb, searching for his driver. The sidewalk was busy, people rushing past him. Some of them glanced his way, but Zeke tended to stand out in a crowd. At six-four, he was packed with muscle. Not all bodyguards were his size. A lot of the agents he employed were able to blend in, to go unnoticed. That would never be the case with Zeke. In addition to his stature, his mixed heritage made him identifiable, too. He was Samoan and Choctaw from his dad's side and white from his mom's.

He located his driver, and within no time, he was riding in the back of a Lincoln, en route to the Hollywood Hills, where Margot lived. They'd sold the Redondo Beach house they'd owned together. Nonetheless, Zeke still lived in that area, making an oceanfront condo his current home.

About forty-five minutes later, he arrived at Margot's residence, an elegant three-bedroom, four-bath Spanish Colonial Revival surrounded by a wrought iron gate.

Zeke instructed his driver to wait for him, then exited the car. He opened the coded gate and ascended the red clay steps leading to the front door. He had a key to her house, but he never used it. It was strictly for security purposes.

Zeke and his partner operated Z-One Security, a personal protection company with over three hundred employees guarding celebrities all over the world. Whenever they took on a new or complicated assignment, Zeke would spend some time with the client, becoming familiar with their lifestyle and training the rest of his team accordingly.

He rang the bell, and Margot answered, looking soft and luscious in a billowy blouse and wide-legged jeans. He noticed that her nails were decorated in mismatched polish. She'd always had an eclectic fashion sense, with different looks to suit whatever type of mood she was in. Today, he surmised, she was in a state of uncertainty. Would that work in his favor? Or was he reading too much into it? She'd never been short on contradictions.

"Hi, Zeke." She greeted him with an anxious smile.

"Hey, Margot." He wasn't going to give her the satisfaction of a smile, anxious or otherwise. He was already pissed at himself for wanting her.

She wore her wild red hair in a low-slung ponytail with loose tendrils framing her face. Her bright blue eyes lent her an innocent quality. Her dimples, however, struck a mischievous chord. They'd served her well when she was a child actor playing a precocious character in *The Kid Years*, the family sitcom she'd become known for. She was playing an adult version of that same character now, in a sequel of the old show aptly called *The Grown-up Years*.

The job that had triggered their divorce.

When they'd first started dating, she'd given up acting, only to resume her career after they got married. A move that felt horribly deceptive to Zeke. He'd never wanted a celebrity wife. He'd grown up with a famous mother, and he'd struggled through every minute of it. As a kid, his only salvation had been his mom's security team. They'd provided a sense of stability in an otherwise chaotic environment, shielding his family from the paparazzi and obsessive fans who hounded his mom. For Zeke, becoming a security specialist when he got older was a no-brainer.

Luckily, Margot didn't need much of a security

detail. Aside from the usual internet trolls who harassed celebrities online, there'd never really been any issues. But he wasn't taking any chances. He engaged a crew to monitor her social media accounts and keep an eye on the camera footage outside her house.

He was being filmed right now. Not that it mattered. As far as his employees knew, his visits with her were strictly professional. He hadn't told a living soul that they were lovers. Margot, on the other hand, had blabbed about their affair to Zeke's sister. The two women had been friends since they were kids, and now his sister was privy to his personal shit.

"Are you going to come inside?" Margot asked.

He nodded and entered the house, catching a glimpse of his dark suit and gray striped tie as he passed a mirror in the foyer. He preferred to wear business attire when he traveled. He would change into a pair of board shorts when he got home.

She escorted him to the living room, a space rife with wood floors, beamed ceilings, a stone fireplace and French casement windows. There was a view of the backyard, including a mixed garden, a pool, a spa and an artfully designed patio.

He glanced at the sofa, but he didn't take a seat. Neither did she. Flustered by their ever-present attraction, he shifted his stance. The energy between them was thick and tangled.

Confusing, he thought.

"Can I get you anything?" she asked.

By now, he was itching to kiss her, to touch her, to carry her to the master suite and do wicked things. "What did you have in mind?"

"Coffee, water, beer. Whatever you want."

He raised his eyebrows. "Whatever I want?" He waited a beat. "Surely you know what that is." He kept his voice low, quiet. Seductive, he supposed. He was making his move, scattered as it was.

Her reaction was just as scattered. In fact, she looked downright dizzy, as if being with him one last time had crossed her mind, too. But then she composed herself and said, "I didn't arrange this meeting for us to…"

"I know, but it's been a while since we…" He'd been away on an assignment for what had seemed like forever, eager to see her, to hook up with her again. "Six months to be exact."

"Yes, but that was before the adoption was finalized and Liam came to live with me."

Zeke had been wondering if this was about her son. The eight-year-old who'd become her priority. He didn't know young Liam, but he'd seen plenty of pictures. He had a security file on the boy.

In all honesty, the idea of her becoming a mom twisted him up inside. Once upon a time, they'd talked about having kids of their own. Of course, that was when they'd been madly in love. But those feelings no longer applied.

Zeke cleared the scratchiness from his throat.

Now that her kid had become part of the discussion, he was at a loss for words. Margot was silent, as well. But that was typical of them. Aside from getting naked, they didn't know how to communicate anymore. Their sexual escapades didn't even include spending any nights together. They just did the deed, then went their separate ways, like hot-blooded strangers hungry for a fix.

Suddenly, he needed a cold drink, something to take the edge off. "If your offer is still good, I think I'd like a beer."

"No problem." She gazed at his mouth, wetting her own lips in the process. "I'm thirsty, too. I'm going to get myself some water." She headed toward the kitchen. "I'll be right back."

Zeke watched her dash out of the room. In spite of the obvious tension, she was trying to act casual. But that did little to ease his mind—or his relentless desire for her.

Margot entered the kitchen and caught her breath. Why did ending her affair with Zeke have to be so painful? Why did she have to want him so badly?

She filled a glass with water from the fridge and drank half of it, telling herself to relax. She could do this. She could let Zeke go for good. It wasn't healthy for her to keep sleeping with him. For now, she needed to focus on her son. Liam was at school today. He was a great student, a smart boy who'd learned to adapt to whatever situation he was in. But his life, thus far, hadn't been easy. He'd spent most of his youth bouncing in and out of foster homes, hoping for a forever family. And now he had Margot.

She'd never intended to become a single parent, but when she'd met Liam at a children's charity, she'd connected with him instantly and knew he was meant to be hers.

She used to think that Zeke was meant to be hers, too, but their divorce had proved otherwise. And their affair? That was insanity. Who slept with their ex instead of moving on? Someday, when she was ready, she would start dating again. But next time she would have a normal relationship, not the turmoil she'd endured with Zeke.

She put her glass in the sink and almost left the kitchen without his beer. *Good Lord.* She grabbed it and returned to the living room. She handed him the bottle, and they both sat. He took the sofa, and she scooted onto an overstuffed chair. He opened the beer and took a long, hard swallow.

He met her gaze, and her heart banged against her ribs. He was a breathtaking man, imposing in his size, with rugged features and eyes that were nearly as black as his hair.

"Where's your water?" he asked.

"I drank it in the kitchen."

"And you're not thirsty anymore?"

"No." At least not for water. Slaking her thirst for him wasn't so easy, but she was determined to exorcise those demons.

She was thirty-three now, and he was thirty-eight. At this point, she'd known him for over half of her life. In addition to her friendship with his sister, she'd also had a close association with his dad. Caine Mitchell used to be Margot's agent. Her own father had walked away when she was seven, abandoning her without a care. She understood that Zeke's childhood was difficult on account of how famous his mother was. But she used to love hanging out at his parents' house and seeing them together. The Hollywood agent and the Hollywood star. They'd been a good match, even if their union had first stemmed from tragedy.

Zeke wasn't Caine's biological son. His birth father was a stuntman who'd been killed in a work-related accident soon after Zeke was born, leaving his mother devastated. In the midst of her grief, she'd married Caine, and he'd adopted her infant son. Bailey had come along five years later, making her Zeke's half sister. Caine was gone now, too. He'd died twelve years ago, leaving an emotional legacy behind. He was the glue that had held everyone together, and they all missed him terribly. Even Margot still brought flowers to his grave.

She looked into Zeke's eyes, those deep, dark hypnotic eyes. To keep things from getting too quiet, she said, "I was just thinking about Caine and how he adopted you."

"And now you have an adopted son." A muscle ticked in his jaw. "But you always wanted kids."

Margot's chest went tight. He'd wanted them, too. Before their marriage had gone awry, they'd talked about having babies. "Becoming a mom has been amazing. But it's still so new and different, and I'm still learning, figuring things out as I go."

"That's normal, I suspect. But I wouldn't really know anything about it." After an uncomfortable pause, he asked, "Are you going to hire a nanny or an au pair? If you are, I need to screen your applicants. Me or one of my agents."

"I'm not going to hire anyone. My mom enjoys watching Liam. She's available whenever I need her. Or she has been so far."

"That's good," he replied, pinning her with his gaze. He swigged his beer without breaking eye contact.

Margot tried not to fidget under his scrutiny. The way he was looking at her made her want to take him straight to bed. But she couldn't, she reminded herself. Not unless she was willing to get all jumbled up again.

Before she did something stupid, she said, "When I texted you last night and said that I was having second thoughts about our affair, I was still struggling with my decision. There was a part of me that wanted to hang on." A part that still did, she thought. Even now, her traitorous body ached for his. "But I need to create a healthy environment for myself and Liam, and I don't see how that's possible if I'm still sleeping with you."

He set his drink on the coffee table. "Then, this is it? It's over?"

"Yes." It had to be, she told herself. No more heart-thundering sex. No more lusty rendezvous.

He leaned back, his massive body sinking into the sofa. "I'm going to miss being with you."

"I'll miss being with you, too." She wasn't going to lie or pretend otherwise. "This wasn't an easy decision."

"Then maybe you shouldn't end it so soon. We can keep doing it for a while and see how it goes. Being a mom doesn't mean you're not allowed to have a lover."

"I know. But I'm trying to do the right thing, and sneaking off with you isn't going to help my cause. There's no future in it. We're divorced," she reminded him.

"I'm well aware of our relationship status." He tugged at his tie, as if the perfectly tied knot was starting to choke him. "But I never would've filed the papers if you'd held up your end of the bargain. When we first got together, you told me that you were done with acting. But then you took that damned sequel. Your old producer called, and you went running."

She narrowed her eyes, irked that he was inciting the same old argument, spinning the narrative to suit him. "I had a right to change my mind. Being an actor makes me happy."

"Oh, really? Then why were you so miserable half the time?"

"I was only miserable when it wasn't going well." She'd made it big at nine years old, and by the time her stardom had ended, she was a teenager, struggling to find her footing. A phase that had lasted through her twenties, when she'd fallen head over heels in love with him. A mistake, if there ever was one. "Everyone else wanted me to succeed again. My mom, your family. Everyone except you." She glared at him. "You're the least supportive person I know."

He loosened his tie all the way. "I supported you plenty. Besides, you knew that I never wanted to be married to a celebrity. That it was a deal breaker for me."

She huffed out a breath. "You didn't even try to compromise."

"Damn it, Margot, I wanted a conventional life with you. Not all of the TV-star hoopla."

"It's not hoopla. It's my job," she shot back.

"A job you chose over me."

"I didn't choose it over you. I wanted my old career back. But you refused to listen to my side of it."

"You didn't care about my side of it, either."

"Yes, I did." She'd taken his issues into consideration. She'd stressed and worried about his feelings. But she'd been foolish in believing that he'd loved her enough to make it work. "You divorced me, not the other way around."

"What was the point of staying together if all we did was fight? I did you a favor by leaving."

She mocked him. "Lucky me, having such a considerate husband. But you know what? You need to go now."

"Gladly." He stood, coming to his towering height.

At five-nine, Margot was considered tall, too. But with his size and strength, he was Hulk material. She used to tease him and say that she was going to paint him green. Now she just wanted to knock him flat on his ass.

He polished off the rest of his beer. "I'll bet that after I'm gone, you're going to run right over to Bailey's and bitch to her about me."

"I can share my feelings with her if I want to." She wasn't going to let him control her friendship with his sister.

"This is bullshit."

"If you say so." She gestured to the front door, but he didn't leave. Instead, he went into the kitchen to rinse out the empty bottle and put it in the recycling container below the sink.

She dogged him. "Look at you. Mr. Tidy."

"So, I'm not a slob. Not like you."

Margot gritted her teeth. "I'm not a slob. A little disorganized, maybe. But that's not the same as being messy."

"Are you kidding? You never clean up after yourself." He glanced at her sparkling counters. "At least you have a great maid service. It's obvious they were here this morning."

"Whatever." It was true, her housekeeper had been there. "Just get out of my sight and don't ever come back."

He rounded on her. "Are you sure you don't want to kiss me first? Or rip off my clothes and claw the crap out of me?"

Her pulse zipped through her body, going straight to the instant heat between her legs. A half-cocked smile spread across his lips. Could he tell that she was turned on by what he'd said? His security training made him a bit of an expert in that regard. He was good at reading people's emotions. Of course, he used to say that she was sometimes hard to gauge. A fact that both challenged and perplexed him.

She lifted her chin. "I never should've had an affair with you."

He stared her down. "Yeah, well, it's too late. You already did."

He didn't immediately leave like he was supposed to. He stayed put, keeping her hanging on by a thread. There was no way she was going to kiss him, or unclothe him, even if she wanted to. Idiot that she was, she would probably fantasize about him tonight: sighing, moaning, touching herself.

"This isn't fair," she said.

"What isn't? That you still want me? Or that I still want you? I wish I knew how to fix it."

"Me, too. It would be nice if we could find a way

to get past it without being so angry." She searched his gaze, desperate for a solution. Neither of them should be suffering this way. "There's got to be something we can do." She studied him, her mind whirring. "Maybe we can try to be friends."

"Friends?" he parroted.

"Yes, you know. A platonic relationship between people who are supposed to like each other."

"Do you like me, Margot?"

"Sometimes," she replied honestly.

"I like you sometimes, too," he said softly.

She always got a little woozy when he whispered. To combat the feeling, she squared her shoulders. "We can use that as our starting point."

He looked worried, dragging a hand through his hair and spiking the short, thick strands.

"Do you really think that'll work?" he asked.

"I don't know." She wasn't any better at being his friend than he was at being hers. "But it's got to be less stressful than fighting." Or wanting each other, she thought. She needed to stomp out her hunger for him. To crush it to bits.

"I guess we can try. But how are we supposed to go about it?"

"I can come by your place on my way to the studio tomorrow morning and bring breakfast." That seemed friendly enough. Plus, her mom was already scheduled to take Liam to school that day. Margot didn't have to alter her routine to see Zeke. "We can figure out where to go from there. But I'll be there really early, so don't sleep in."

"Do I ever?"

"No, I suppose not." He was an early riser, a habit that had been formed from surfing. He used any excuse to hit the waves. Sometimes he even paddled out on moonlit nights.

He squinted. "I better go now, before we start arguing again and blow this whole deal."

"Good call." She agreed that it was safer for him to leave while they were on a positive note.

She walked him to the door, and the moment turned awkward. He leaned forward to hug her, but then he pulled back, as if it might not be a very platonic thing to do. In their case, he was right to keep his distance. She didn't need to feel his big, broad body next to hers.

"I'll see you tomorrow," he said.

"You, too." She watched him descend the steps and retreat to the town car waiting for him.

Was initiating a friendship with him the smartest course of action? She wasn't altogether sure, but she'd already made the offer, and she was going to follow through.

No matter how difficult it proved to be.

Two

After Zeke left, Margot headed over to Bailey's house. He'd been right about her wanting to see his sister. But she wasn't going there to bitch. She needed a bit of girl talk.

Bailey was a screenwriter who worked predominantly from home, and as long as she wasn't on a pressing deadline, she made herself available to Margot.

They both lived in the Hollywood Hills, only in different neighborhoods. Margot resided in Whitley Heights, a historic district built during the rise of the motion picture industry, and Bailey was in Laurel Canyon, a mountainous area rooted in the 1960s and '70s counterculture.

Margot took the winding road that led to Bailey's house, a woodsy cabin perched on a hill, surrounded by herbs, flowers and dense foliage. Zeke's sister valued her privacy, something she shared with her brother. Neither of them had basked in the spotlight of their mother's fame. Zeke had reacted to it by building a personal protection empire, and Bailey took refuge in the isolation of writing.

Margot liked being in the public eye. She enjoyed posing for pictures and chatting with fans and walking red carpets. She was nowhere near as famous as Eva Mitchell, though. Zeke and Bailey's mother had been a world-renowned sex symbol in her day. Even now, she was still revered for her beauty.

Margot parked on Bailey's narrow street and made her way to the back of the cabin. Bailey said that she would be working outside today.

Sure enough, there she was curled up in a hammock with her laptop. She didn't look anything like Zeke. She didn't have his tense personality, either. Bailey was a petite, blue-eyed blonde with an easy nature. She sported a casual style, too. Sometimes she dressed up, but mostly she gravitated to sweats and sneakers, or cutoff shorts and sandals.

"I'm here," Margot announced.

"I know." Bailey glanced over and grinned. "I saw you out of the corner of my eye." She closed her laptop and got to her feet.

Margot moved toward her for a hug. Bailey always smelled so soft and natural. In her spare time, she concocted soaps and lotions and organic potions.

They embraced, and Bailey said, "I made lemonade." She gestured to the fruit trees in her yard. "Fresh from the source."

"Thanks. I'll try to make this visit short."

"No problem. I have time." Bailey removed the lemonade from a boxy little fridge in the entertainment area. She poured two glasses and placed them on a wood table surrounded by chairs decorated with floral-printed cushions.

They sat across from each other. On this bright spring day, the sun shined gloriously over the hills. In the silence that followed, Bailey tucked a strand of her honey-colored hair behind her ear. The silky strands were so long, they skimmed her tailbone. Margot had to work a lot harder on her hair, thick and wavy as it was, putting product on it to keep it from frizzing. But the unruliness suited her, so she didn't mind.

She gave herself another reflective second to breathe before she said, "I broke off my affair with Zeke."

"Oh, wow. You did it. You actually did it." Bailey paused. "I loved having you as my sister-in-law, and I wished your marriage would've worked, but I'm relieved that you finally ended that crazy affair."

"I knew you would be. You kept telling me how emotionally damaging you thought it was for me to keep sleeping with him."

"I told Zeke the same thing. In my opinion, it wasn't good for either of you. Of course, as hard-headed as my brother is, he wouldn't listen to a thing I had to say." She leaned forward. "How did he take it?"

"Not well at first. We got into an argument over the past, but then we decided to try to be friends."

Bailey's eyes went wide. "You both decided that?"

"It was my suggestion, but he agreed to give it a go. I'm going to stop by his condo tomorrow to talk more about it."

"No offense, but you better not end up back in his bed."

"No offense taken. And for the record, he tried to get me to be with him today, but I turned him down."

"I'm glad to hear it. But just be careful, okay? Old habits and all of that."

Old habits, indeed. Their affair had started on an evening where they'd met up to discuss business. She'd wanted to use a different security service after the divorce, but he'd insisted that she stay with his company. At some point, they'd gotten into a raging fight that had culminated in a wild bout of sex. "I swear, I'm not going to do anything stupid."

Bailey laughed a little. "Well, I think you being his friend sounds kind of stupid."

Margot laughed, too. But only for a moment. Turning serious, she said, "There came a point when he made the choice to stop loving me, and when I stopped loving him, too. But we never got closure after the divorce. Instead, we just kept sleeping together."

"So, if you learn to become friends, you'll both get the closure you need?"

"It's worth a try." Margot sipped her lemonade. "Remember that crush I had on him when we were kids?"

Bailey crinkled her nose. "How could I forget? He was all you ever talked about. I wanted to jump off a bridge whenever you cooed his name."

"I know. I'm sorry for putting you through that. But the first time I saw him, so tall and dark and broody, I nearly melted on the spot. He wasn't nearly as impressed with me."

"He thought you were a pest back then."

"I was, I suppose. A gangly fourteen-year-old, fresh from a canceled sitcom, mooning over my best friend's brother. He was a freshman in college, and there I was, giggling and acting silly, trying to get his attention."

"You finally got old enough for him to take an interest in you."

"Sometimes I think it would have been easier if we'd never gotten together at all. Having a crush on him was bad enough, but the way I loved him later on…"

His sister sighed. "Yes, but look at you now. A strong and successful single mom. I'm proud of how far you've come."

"Thank you. I appreciate you saying that." And once she tackled this friendship thing with Zeke, she intended to become even stronger, conquering her hunger for him for good.

The following morning, Margot was on her way, ready to face Zeke. She stopped at a trendy food truck near his place that specialized in healthy meals and gourmet coffee. The female server recognized her and asked for a selfie. She happily obliged, flashing her best smile.

She returned to her car and continued her journey. The home she and Zeke used to own together wasn't far from here, but she avoided going down that street. She didn't need the reminder that they were once married.

Zeke's modern-style condo faced the ocean. After she arrived, she approached his private deck, a low-maintenance area with a fire ring, a grouping of lounge chairs and a mosaic-topped table. He could've afforded to buy her out and keep their other house, but he'd decided to start over somewhere new. Hence, this cool, sleek bachelor pad.

She set everything down and rang the bell. She waited, but he didn't answer. Had he slept in after all? She tried a second time. Then a third. Seriously, how tired could he be?

She fired off a text. I'm outside your door. Where are you?

Again, she waited. But he didn't reply.

At this point, she was getting downright miffed. Zeke used to say that her fiery disposition matched her hair. But today she had good reason for being mad. She'd come all this way, only to be shunned by him.

She turned to gather the bags and leave, when she spotted him on the beach with his surfboard propped in the sand. She hadn't even thought to look for him out there, even if it was the most logical place for him to be.

As she watched him peel off his wetsuit, her heart began to pound. He was wearing shorts underneath, but just the act of him undressing was enough to send her into a tailspin.

He turned and noticed her. They stared at each other from across the distance. He headed in her direction, and she unpacked the food, setting up their meal on the table.

When he got closer, she noticed how tight his shorts were. Well, of course they were snug. They were Lycra. He never wore board shorts under his wetsuit; they bunched too much.

"I'm sorry if I kept you waiting," he said.

She was doing her damnedest not to drool. All that brawny muscle. All that masculine beauty. Was it any wonder that she'd kept sleeping with him after the divorce? "I texted you. But I didn't realize that you were on the beach."

"I didn't bring my phone with me. Do you want to come in while I get dressed?"

"No, thanks. I'll stay here." She didn't want to be anywhere near him when he took off those skin-tight shorts. She was already struggling to block that image from her wayward mind.

He gripped his board. "I'm not going to shower. I can do that later."

She actually would've preferred that he showered. To her, the scent of the sea on his skin was just another aphrodisiac. "You don't have to rush on my account."

"But I kept you waiting. I'm just going to put on some clothes. I'll be right back."

He entered the condo, leaving her alone with her thoughts. She sipped her coffee and gazed out at the ocean, trying to stay calm. Her mind was still misbehaving. She couldn't stop thinking about his body-hugging shorts. The surfer-boy smell of his skin. The affair she was already missing.

He returned, dressed in faded jeans, a dark blue pullover and slip-on sneakers. Margot was wearing a standard gray hoodie. It was a chilly spring morning, but it was supposed to warm up later.

"How long do we have?" he asked.

She blinked. "What?"

"Before you have to leave for the studio."

She checked her phone for the time. "About thirty minutes." Which seemed like an eternity now.

He sat across from her. "Thank you for this. I'm starving. I don't have any groceries in the house. I plan to go shopping later, though."

She watched him attack his food. They were having the same thing to eat: egg-and-cheese burritos, sautéed sweet potatoes and fresh fruit. Their drinks were different. Hers was a café mocha, and his was a dead eye: a regular coffee with three shots of espresso. She knew his tastes. The man definitely liked it strong.

He finished chewing a mouthful of burrito and gulped his coffee. "Can I ask you something that I've been wondering about for a while?" He placed his cup back on the table. "Have you been with anyone else, besides me, since the divorce?"

Margot nearly flinched. That was what he was curious about? Other partners? "We agreed back then that our affair wasn't going to be exclusive."

"Yeah, but now that it's over, I was hoping it would be okay to talk more about it."

Stalling, she took a small bite of her potatoes. She hadn't been with anyone else, but she didn't want him to perceive it as loyalty. Or some sort of misguided feelings for him that still lingered.

Rather than respond to his question, she turned it around on him. "What about you? How many women were you with while you were sleeping with me?"

He answered outright. "None. It seemed too complicated to be having an affair with you and be seeing other people, too."

"It was the same for me. You were the only one.

But now neither of us has to worry about that complication anymore."

They just needed to learn to quit lusting after each other.

He took another bite of his burrito. Then he asked, "Does Liam know that you're divorced?"

More personal questions, she thought. More discomfort. "Yes, but I only mentioned it to him in passing. I didn't go into the specifics, other than I used to be married to Bailey's brother and that you own the company that provides our security." Which seemed specific enough, she realized. "I wouldn't have said anything to him at all, but he's really close to your sister, so I thought it might come up at some point anyway. He adores Bailey. She's one of his favorite people."

Zeke drank more of his coffee, gazing at her from across the rim of his cup. "How did they get so close?"

"Aside from her being my best friend?" Most people would have assumed the obvious, Margot thought. But not her analytical ex. He was always looking for deeper meanings. And in this case, he was right. "Bailey has been helping Liam write a children's book that they're going to self-publish. It's about a dog that adopts orphaned kittens. The concept was his idea. He's really excited about it. He wants to give the proceeds from the book to the foster charity that helped him and me become a family."

"That must make you proud." Zeke seemed impressed by her son's sensitivity. But there was something else, too. Something she couldn't quite name. Until he said, "I'd like to meet Liam. I'd like to get to know him."

"For security reasons or on a personal level?"

"Both, if that's okay with you."

"Can I think about it?" She wanted to be careful not to rush into anything. "You and I are just starting to get to know each other again, and I don't want to confuse Liam by introducing him to you too soon."

"Just let me know what you decide. I'll be around for a while. In fact, I'm taking the next month or so off. My last assignment was pretty grueling, and I need to relax before I jump back into another one."

As a small breeze kicked up, she tucked her napkin under her food container to keep it from blowing away. "I'll be free soon, too. Once we wrap up this season, we won't start filming again until the show is officially renewed by the network."

"Then it sounds like we have plenty of time to see each other." He grabbed his napkin before it took flight. "And do whatever friends do."

She glanced at her phone, suddenly eager to leave. Zeke was studying her a bit too closely, reminding her of the past, of the pain, of the children they should've had together. "I should probably get going." She closed her food container. "I'll take the rest of this with me."

"Has it been thirty minutes already?"

She rose from her seat. "No, but it's close

enough." And she needed to get her emotions back on track. She didn't want to show up at work all rattled.

He walked her to the edge of the deck, and they stood a few torturous feet apart. His proximity made her want to kiss him, to taste his luscious mouth, to press herself against him.

"You can go take your shower now," she said, as the wind whipped between them. "Not that you need my permission," she quickly added. "I was just…"

"I know…" He hesitated. "I'll wait to hear from you about when we should get together again. Or when I can meet Liam or whatever happens next."

Margot pushed a strand of hair away from her face. Would she be stronger the next time she saw him? She hoped so. If not, she was just going to have to keep trying, for however long it took.

Margot spent the evening with her mom and Liam. After Liam went to bed, she and her mom went back to the kitchen so Margot could clean up.

She made a point to load the dishwasher rather than leave the dinner dishes in the sink the way she sometimes did.

But mostly she was stealing glances at her powerhouse mom.

Sixty-five-year-old June Jensen was a sturdy brunette who loved the entertainment industry with a vengeance. She'd hired Caine to be Margot's agent while she'd managed Margot's career, but she was happily retired now and living in an active fifty-five-plus community with other Hollywood diehards. At the moment, she stood at the counter with a pair of rhinestone readers perched on the end of her nose and the latest copy of *People* magazine at her fingertips. She still liked to read the old-school way, flipping through the glossy pages until she got to the cover story. Margot had never been on the cover of *People*, but she'd been featured inside, something that had thrilled her mom to no end.

Typically, nothing fazed June. Or that was the impression she gave. Margot knew otherwise. Her mother had been devastated when Margot's daddy up and left, crying herself to sleep on long, lonely nights.

Margot had cried, too. She'd spent years thinking it was her fault, that if she'd been a better daughter, he would have stuck around. Even before he left, he'd seemed indifferent, leaving her longing for his affection. Once she'd landed *The Kid Years*, she'd been certain that he would come back to be part of her life. Only he never did. He'd made his child support payments on time, but that was where their connection ended. These days, he was remarried and living in Costa Rica with his much younger wife. He had absolutely nothing to do with Margot. He didn't even follow her on social media.

Her mom, on the other hand, was her biggest fan. She'd gotten Margot into the business when she was just a baby. To some people June had seemed like a

typical stage mom, pushing and prodding and trying to make her kid a star. But for Margot, the attention had felt good, especially with her dad's lack
of interest.

It was strange how her celebrity affected her family. Her mother loved it, her father didn't care, Liam
thought it was cool and Zeke had divorced her over
it.

Of course, now she had the pressing issue of
being his friend and deciding how and when to introduce him to Liam.

"Can I talk to you about something?" she asked
her mom. At this point, she wanted her mother's advice, even if she was only going to give her bits and
pieces of the story.

"Sure. What is it?" Her mom removed her glasses
and set the magazine aside, settling in for their discussion.

"I had breakfast with Zeke this morning. But it
wasn't a security meeting. He and I are working toward being friends."

Her mom cocked her head, her hair falling at a
blunt angle against her chin. "I know you've maintained a business rapport since the divorce. But you
want to be friends now?"

Margot nodded. "We thought that we could hang
out and do a few things together." Except for being
lovers, she thought. But she couldn't mention that
part.

"Well, there's certainly nothing wrong with socializing with him. Lots of exes in this town do that. It's more common than people think. But I'm curious why you sound so trepidatious. He's not pressuring you, is he?"

"Not at all. It was my idea. But I do have some concerns about Liam. Zeke wants me to introduce them, and I'm afraid that it might confuse Liam to see me hanging around with Zeke."

"Confuse him how? You're a single adoptive mom, making an effort to be friends with your ex-husband. I think that's a healthy approach to divorce and a positive lesson to teach your child. Granted, Zeke hurt you when he walked away. But you were smart enough to get over him."

Smart? Margot would've laughed if she didn't feel so utterly dumb right now. "You're right. I'm probably making a bigger deal out of it than it is. Maybe I'll text Zeke tonight and try to set something up for him and Liam to meet over the weekend." At least then she could quit fretting over it.

Her mother leaned against the counter. "I admire you for being a modern woman and approaching this the way you are. And as much as I disapprove of the way Zeke ended your marriage, I appreciate that he still cares about keeping you safe. You shouldn't have a problem hanging out."

"I'm glad you see it that way." She summoned a hurried smile. "I hope us being friends works in our favor." Far more than she could possibly explain. "But maybe I should get back to the dishes now."

She didn't want to talk this to death or slip up and give herself away, revealing that she still had sexual feelings for Zeke.

No matter how hard she tried not to.

Three

On Wednesday afternoon, while Zeke was at his mom's house, he called and checked in with his partner at the office. Although Zeke had started Z-One Security with his share of the money that he and Bailey had inherited from their dad, he hadn't done it alone. He'd recruited Vick Rossi, one of his mom's old bodyguards, to join him.

"How's Eva doing?" Vick asked.

"I don't know," Zeke replied. "She hasn't come downstairs yet." He was in the parlor, waiting for his illustrious mother to join him.

"What about Bailey?" Vick asked.

"She's not here yet, either." The three of them had arranged to visit today, but he was the only one on time. Was this how Margot had felt when she'd showed up at his door and he wasn't there?

"Your mom is probably still putting on her face and deciding what to wear, and your sister will probably rush in with a messy braid and smudged mascara."

"That sounds about right." Those two women had absolutely nothing in common. Eva was a glamour queen who'd been dubbed the sex kitten of her era, and Bailey was anything but. "You know my family well."

"I cared for them like my own."

"You most certainly did." Vick had protected the Mitchells with his life. He was in his seventies now and had contacts in every sector of law enforcement. He made a damned fine partner for Zeke.

"I'll bet you're really missing your dad on days like this," Vick said.

"That's for sure." Zeke loved his mother and sister, but sometimes their energy drove him crazy. "I'm going to hang up now and pour myself a drink."

"Enjoy it while you can."

"Will do." He ended the call and approached the bar. He chose a single-malt scotch and added a dash of spring water. His dad had taught him that water helped bring out the aroma of the scotch.

As he sipped his drink, he sank into a chair and glanced around the lavish room. His mom favored French furniture, ornamental pieces designed for a king and his court. Or a queen and her court in her case. She definitely lived like a royal. There'd been a throng of housekeepers and cooks and assistants who'd worked here over the years. Some of the most loyal still remained.

Overall, the estate rested on five acres, with an eighteen-bedroom, twenty-four-bathroom main house, a guesthouse, a guardhouse and a ten-car garage. When Zeke was a kid, his favorite part of the mansion had been the game room. He'd spent plenty of time in the pool and spa, too, soaking up the Southern California sun.

He'd hated going out in public with his parents. He'd relied on Vick and the rest of his mom's security team to make those occasions more bearable. Red carpet events used to be his greatest nightmare. His mom would drag him and Bailey to them whenever she'd starred in a PG-rated movie that she thought was age-appropriate for them to see. She'd made a handful of madcap comedies, where she played the dumb blonde. At least those silly things were tolerable. What bothered Bailey the most were the nude magazine spreads. Zeke had learned to let those roll off his back. But since he was a guy, people didn't compare him to Eva or pick him apart, not like they did to Bailey. He'd always felt bad for his sister because of that.

Footsteps echoed on the polished wood floors, signaling that someone was headed toward the parlor. He knew it was his mom, even before he saw her. He recognized the click of her high heels.

He stood to greet her, and she moved forward, reaching out to embrace him. Even as tender as their hug was, he was still careful not to press too hard and wrinkle her outfit. A habit from his youth.

They separated, and he took a moment to analyze her appearance. At sixty-two, she was as shapely as she'd ever been, courtesy of a private trainer and her dedication to yoga. Her platinum hair was still bleached to perfection, and she was still capable of giving smoldering looks to a camera, even if she wasn't required to do that anymore.

Although she'd aged well, she hadn't aged naturally. She got regular Botox treatments. She'd had plenty of little nips and tucks, too. Today she was wearing a silky pink dress that matched her lipstick.

"You look amazing, Mom," he said, feeding her delicate ego. She'd always needed a lot of attention. But she also had a kind and giving heart. She volunteered at women's shelters and donated millions to the cause.

"My handsome and brilliant son." She touched his cheek. "You look so much like your other daddy."

She was referring to his birth father, the stuntman who'd died when Zeke was a baby. But at least he knew his "other" daddy's family. He'd been visiting his paternal grandfather in Samoa since he was a kid. He loved it there.

"Can I fix you a drink?" he asked, taking charge of the bar.

"I'll just have some cranberry juice."

He poured it over ice then handed her the glass. "To the lady of the manor," he said, toasting her with his scotch.

"I'll drink to that." She sipped her juice. "Where is that sister of yours? I thought she'd be here by now."

"You know Bailey. She marches to the beat of her own drum."

"I worry about what a recluse she is."

"She has Margot to keep her company. Those two will always be as thick as thieves." Far thicker than he would've liked.

"So it seems." Eva stood beside the white marble fireplace with intricate scrolls and a curved base, almost as if she was posing next to it, her shoulder resting against the lightly veined mantel. "Have you seen her?"

He finished his scotch. "What? Who?"

"Margot. Have you seen her since you got back?"

"Yes, but we always touch base whenever I come home. For business and whatnot," he added. The "whatnot" used to be sex. Hot, secret sex. Or almost secret. It still irked him that his sister knew about the affair. She'd even had the gall to tell him how much she disapproved of it. "Margot is supposed to introduce me to her son this weekend." She'd already texted him with the day and time, moving faster than he'd anticipated.

"I haven't met him yet. Bailey says that he's a doll. They're working on a children's book together."

"Yeah. Margot told me about that." Zeke was anxious about meeting Liam, but he sure as hell wasn't going to let it show.

"It's nice that you and Margot are on decent terms. Considering how volatile the end of your marriage was, I never thought you'd speak to each other again."

"We got past that." By tearing each other's clothes off, he thought. "We're trying to be better friends now." *Better* made it sound as if they already were friends, but his mom didn't seem to notice. She wasn't as observant as Bailey.

Speaking of his meddlesome sibling, she finally came dashing around the corner and into the parlor. She wore her ultralong hair in a flyaway braid, just as Vince had predicted. Her mascara wasn't smeared, but that was only because she wasn't wearing any makeup.

"Bonjour, Maman." She greeted their mother in French, using the language in affectionate jest, poking fun at the furniture. When Bailey was little, she'd gotten into trouble for scribbling on a console table in this very room.

A second later, she smiled at Zeke and said, "Hey, big brother."

He raised his eyebrows. "What? No foreign language for me?"

She hugged him instead, taking the opportunity to whisper in his ear. "It's the only running joke I have with Mom."

That was true. Most of her interactions with their mom were strained. "Are you happy now that Margot ended things with me?" he whispered back, chiding her for getting involved in his affair. She was the last person who should've been doling out relationship advice. She'd never been married. Hell, she'd never even had a serious boyfriend.

Bailey pulled away from him before their mother could notice that something was amiss. It was all Zeke could do not to glower at his sister. She grabbed his glass and sniffed it.

"Maybe I should have one of these," she said. "Will you fix it for me?"

Yeah, whatever, he thought. He walked over to the bar.

"Make it a double," she called after him. "No, wait, on second thought, I'll have a ginger ale, a splash of grenadine and two cherries."

He rolled his eyes. She'd just requested a Shirley Temple, her beverage of choice when they were kids. He mixed her mocktail and made his next scotch a double.

After the three of them settled in to chat, Eva said, "Just so you know, I'm scheduled for surgery on the twenty-fourth."

Bailey reacted with a start. "Oh, my goodness, why? What's wrong?"

"Nothing is wrong," their mother quickly replied. "I'm having my implants replaced."

Zeke figured it was something like that. Bailey should've assumed as much, too.

"Really?" his sister asked. "Another boob job?"

"Don't get all testy about it. They're supposed to be replaced every ten years. This time, I'm having them lifted, too."

Bailey sighed. "If you're going to all that trouble, then why don't you just have them removed?"

"Because I'm used to having implants. Besides, at my age, why should I have to compromise? My own aren't nearly as big."

Zeke all but winced. This wasn't a conversation he wanted to be part of. He walked over to a window, letting the women hash it out.

He opened the drapes and gazed out at a picturesque view of the garden maze. The elaborate design had been inspired by the labyrinth of Versailles. It had also been the site of his and Margot's wedding. She'd looked like a princess that day, draped in a beaded gown. She'd even worn a tiara with a veil attached. He'd felt like the luckiest guy in the world, lifting that veil, kissing her, claiming his bride.

And now they weren't even lovers anymore.

Would their friendship prove futile, too? He didn't have a clue what to think. But it wasn't helping, getting wrapped up in that damned maze. He closed the drapes, shutting it out.

He tuned back into the squabble his mother and sister were having. By now, Eva had conned Bailey into staying with her for a couple of days after the surgery, even if she already had a house full of people to look after her. But that was how their disagreements typically went, with Bailey losing the battle. Zeke moved away from the window and rejoined them.

A short time later, their visit ended. Their mother retreated to her suite to relax, and Zeke and Bailey exited the mansion together.

They lingered in the circular driveway. She was at least a foot shorter than him, so it was easy to peer down at her.

"Why do you even bother arguing with Mom?" he asked.

"Someone has to. Besides, it's easier than arguing with you." When he blew out a flustered breath, she said, "Come on now, don't be mad at me over you and Margot. It was her decision to end your affair, not mine."

"Yeah, but you kept encouraging her to do it."

"That's only because I didn't want to see either of you get hurt." She squinted as the sun got in her eyes. "Truthfully, I would've preferred seeing you stay married. But you're the one who destroyed that."

"She destroyed it first." But he wasn't going to stand here and battle with his baby sister over the emotional schematics of why he'd gotten divorced. "I need to go. I have things to do." That was a lie. The rest of his day was free. He just wanted to escape with his emotions intact.

"Okay, but don't be mad at me," she said again.

"I'm not, I guess." Deep down, he knew that she only had his best interest at heart. But that didn't help ease his frustration over Margot. The woman he'd married in a maze, he thought. The ex-wife who still consumed him.

Margot sat next to Liam at the dining room table, watching him create a submarine with one of his Lego sets. He was making an entire world under the sea. He loved the ocean and everything in it. Like Zeke, she thought.

Was that the only interest they had in common? Probably, she thought. Whatever the case, she hadn't even told Liam that Zeke was visiting today. But she couldn't withhold that information much longer. Zeke would be there within the hour.

"We're having company soon," Margot said.

"We are?" Her son glanced up from his project, his blondish-brown hair falling onto his forehead. He wore it in a simple style, but he had a couple of cowlicks that could make it tough to manage. His eyes were big and brown, so big, he often reminded her of a saucer-eyed anime character.

"Who's coming over?" he asked.

"Bailey's brother," she quickly answered.

His enormous eyes lit up. "Is Bailey coming, too?"

"No, just Zeke."

His shoulders slumped. "Why isn't she coming?"

"She's working today. Besides, I thought it would be nice if you got to meet Zeke on his own. He used to be my husband, but he's also my friend." Or so she hoped.

Liam set his submarine aside. "What if it gets boring with just me and you and him?"

Being bored was the least of her worries. "Then we'll think of something fun to do."

"What kind of stuff is he into?"

"He lives at the beach, so he loves the ocean. He's an accomplished surfer. It's one of his favorite things to do." She gestured at Liam's creation. "He'll probably think that's cool."

He grabbed one of his Lego fish and made it cruise through the air. "Maybe we can go swimming when he's here."

"Sure, why not?" Anything to make this easier. "I'll text him and tell him to bring his trunks. We can eat by the pool."

"What are we having?"

"Zeke is bringing tacos." He'd insisted on providing lunch. "But I'm going to make some banana pudding for dessert." Her son was a bit of a banana freak. His favorite sandwich was peanut butter and banana. Sometimes she even fried them for him.

He smiled. "I can help you make the pudding, Mom."

Her heart went warm. She loved hearing him call her Mom. He'd started saying it as soon as the adoption was finalized. Although Liam didn't remember his birth mother, he knew that she was gone. That much he'd been told.

Margot knew the details, of course. Daisy had been a troubled, drug-addicted teen from an abusive home. At eighteen, she'd gotten pregnant with Liam. She quit doing drugs and tried to be a good mom, but two years later, she started using again and lost her little boy to foster care. When he was four, she died from an accidental overdose. Liam's father had never been in the picture. He was a hookup from a party and someone Daisy never saw again. But that didn't mean that Liam wasn't curious about his birth parents. Just last week, he'd asked Margot if she had any pictures of them. She couldn't help him with his dad. No one knew his identity. But she gave Liam a photograph of Daisy that she'd gotten a while back from his old caseworker, and he seemed thrilled to have it. He kept it tucked away in his room like a treasure.

Z-One Security had the same picture in their files. Margot had provided Zeke's company with information about Liam. They knew everything there was to know about her son. And about her, too, except for the part where she'd been sleeping with Zeke after the divorce.

She texted him and got an immediate reply. He was totally up for a swim. He included water emojis for effect.

Liam's attention span in the kitchen was short. He helped her slice the bananas, then ran upstairs to change. He was starting to seem excited about Zeke coming over. Or maybe he was just excited about going in the pool.

Margot finished making the pudding and went to her room to slip on her swimsuit. She chose a simple blue bikini with white polka dots. But for now, she covered up with a sundress. She reapplied her lip gloss and fluffed her hair, for whatever that was worth.

She returned to the kitchen and gathered plates, flatware and napkins. After setting the patio table by the pool, she went back inside and waited.

Zeke arrived about ten minutes later with a big bag of food. He was dressed in a pineapple-print shirt, board shorts and flip-flops.

Margot took the bag, while Liam inched forward and stared at the stranger in front of him. For now, they remained in the living room.

"It's nice to meet you," Zeke said, breaking the awkward silence.

"You don't look like you'd be Bailey's brother," Liam replied, still gaping up at him.

Zeke shifted his stance. "I'm her half brother."

"Which half?" the eight-year-old asked.

Zeke glanced at Margot, and they exchanged a smile that made her heart go pitter-pat. She pressed the bag closer to her chest.

"Bailey and I have the same mother," Zeke said to Liam. "But neither of us looks like her. I look like my dad, and Bailey looks like her father."

"I think you look like Aquaman."

"Really?" Zeke bent down to talk to Liam, putting himself at a less intimidating level. "Your mom always told me that if I was green, I would look like the Hulk."

"No." Her son shook his head, quite serious in his assessment. "You're more like Aquaman. Except you don't have long hair and a beard like the guy in the movie. Yours is more like stubble or whatever it's called."

"I don't have his magical trident, either," Zeke said. "But I wish I did."

Liam only nodded. Aquaman was his favorite superhero, and now he seemed starstruck, almost as if Zeke was the real deal. But it was easy to be awed by Zeke. Margot had been that way for years.

"Should we go outside and have our lunch now?" she asked.

"Sure." Zeke moved toward the French doors that led to the backyard and the patio. Liam followed him like a puppy.

When they got to the patio table, Margot unpacked the bag. In addition to the tacos, there were rice and beans, and guacamole and chips.

"What do you guys want to drink?" she asked. "The fridge out here is jammed with sodas and bottled water and juice."

"I'll take a water," Zeke replied.

"Me, too," Liam said, even if he rarely drank

water. He normally wanted something sweet. Her kid definitely had a case of idol worship.

They sat down to eat, and Zeke opened a slew of hot sauce containers—the fiery stuff—and doused his tacos. Margot glanced over at Liam, hoping he didn't mimic Zeke again. Luckily, he didn't. Liam would've gagged on something that hot.

The meal was relatively quiet, but things got noisy in the pool afterward. Liam and Zeke had loads of fun, swimming, splashing and goofing around. Liam was right. Zeke was more Aquaman than Hulk. Liam could've been an Atlantean, too. They both should've been born with fins.

Margot was pleased to see them getting along so well, but deep down, it hurt, too. Zeke would've made a great father, if he'd given their marriage a chance. Only now, she was a single mom watching her son fawn all over her ex.

She decided not to join them in the pool. Instead she sat on the edge of the shallow end, still wearing her sundress and dipping her feet in the water.

"Come in, Mom!" Liam yelled out to her. He and Zeke were playing water basketball, with Zeke lifting Liam up to help him make the shots.

"I'm good where I am."

"Come on!" Liam prodded her again.

She shook her head. "You guys are doing just fine on your own."

"Zeke can make you come in," Liam said. "He's big enough to pull you in the water."

She gazed past Liam and made eye contact with Zeke, cautioning him not to do it.

"I won't pull you in," he said, heeding her silent warning. "But it would be nice if you'd join us."

"*Please.*" Liam begged.

"All right." He deserved a mom who was willing to be part of the fun. Besides, she was supposed to be establishing a friendship with Zeke, not sitting around being tormented by him. "I have to put sunscreen on first."

She walked over to the table, where the lotion was. Then, without a moment's notice, Zeke emerged from the pool with water dripping from his body and puddling at his feet.

"What are you doing?" she asked, under her breath.

"I'm going to help you with the sunscreen."

"I can do it myself."

"You can't get your back by yourself. And that's the part of you that sometimes burns the worst."

So much for not being tormented. Just being near him was giving her goose bumps. She handed him the lotion and peeled off her sundress, holding her breath, anticipating his touch.

Thank goodness Liam wasn't watching. He paddled around the basketball hoop, cheering for himself and pretending to be an NBA star.

As Margot turned to face the pool, Zeke moved to stand behind her. She heard him opening the bottle and squeezing the lotion into his hands, warming it up.

He started at her shoulders and worked his way down, applying the sunscreen in circular motions.

"Just making sure I don't miss a spot," he said.

She couldn't find the words to respond. Every nerve ending in her body came alive, tingling wherever he touched. He went all the way down to her tailbone, and she nearly moaned.

Liam finally looked over at them. "Hurry up, you guys!"

"Almost done," Zeke called back, fumbling just a bit.

Margot felt his fingers slip on her skin, as if he'd just gotten caught doing something horribly forbidden. Which, in a sense, he had. They both knew better.

He came around to hand her the bottle, and they gazed uncomfortably at each other. "I'll let you finish up," he said.

Yes, she would do the rest of her body. But the damage of him touching her had already been done, the intimacy giving rise to carnal urges she couldn't afford to indulge.

He cleared his throat. "I better get back to Liam."

She nodded, wondering how she was going to survive Zeke's company for the rest of the afternoon. One thing was for sure: she was never going to let him put his hands on her like that again.

He dived into the pool, making a huge splash and

getting the ball away from Liam. Her son laughed, and they resumed their game.

Margot slathered on the rest of the sunscreen, putting it everywhere she could reach, protecting herself from the sun. If only there was a lotion that could protect her from Zeke and the scorching heat he incited.

Four

Zeke spent the next hour stealing glances at Margot while she swam and splashed and got beautifully wet. Being around her was painful. But he thrived on it, too. His fingers still tingled from where he'd touched her.

By now they were having races, paddling from one end of the pool to the other on inflatable floats. He'd won two rounds until Margot and Liam cheated and ganged up on him, pushing him straight off his alligator-shaped float.

It was weird, but somewhere in his warped mind, it almost felt as if he and Margot were married again and Liam was their kid. Yet thinking along those lines was ludicrous. Goofing around in the pool with her son didn't make them anything even remotely close to being a family. Zeke was just caught up in the moment, getting dragged into Margot's seductive clutches.

Would he ever get over his desire for her? The fact that neither of them had been with anyone else after the divorce seemed proof that they were both still a bit too tied up with each other.

"Can we have our dessert now?" Liam asked his mom.

"Oh, yes, absolutely." She paddled to the side of the pool on her sparkly mermaid float. Zeke couldn't stop himself from watching her.

She glanced over at him. "Do you want some pudding?"

What he wanted was to eat her alive. He could only imagine how good she would taste.

"Yeah, sure," he said, fighting a frown. "Pudding."

She grabbed a towel and dried off. "I'll bring it to the table."

While she went into the house, he climbed out of the pool and got a canned iced tea from the beverage fridge, needing to cool his libido. He flipped the top and chugged it down, finishing it in two seconds flat.

Liam appeared at his elbow, and he handed him a can, too. Margot's son was a cute little guy, chasing Zeke around like a mini-me. Margot used to chase him around when she was a teenager, but that had been a whole other thing.

She returned, carrying a tray with the pudding. They served themselves, eating out of clear-plastic bowls.

"How long were you guys married?" Liam asked suddenly.

Zeke hadn't expected this line of questioning. Clearly, neither had Margot; she paused midbite. But maybe they should've been better prepared.

A moment later, she replied, "We were married for three years, but we knew each other a long time before that."

Liam had a perplexed expression. "Then how come you got divorced?"

"Sometimes people are better off being friends."

She glanced at Zeke, and he nodded, hoping her statement was true. For now, the friendship angle was still new.

Liam accepted her answer, only to turn to Zeke and ask, "What's it like to own a security company?"

He was surprised but thankful for the change of subject. "I like keeping my clients safe, so it feels good to me. Sometimes I work directly as their bodyguard, but that part isn't always as exciting as it sounds. I spend a lot of time just driving them around, accompanying them on their day-to-day activities."

Young Liam thought about it for a second, then asked, "Have you ever been my mom's bodyguard?"

"No, I haven't." But there were plenty of agents in his company who were available to her. Nonetheless, she used to say that she thought his bodyguard persona was hot. Too bad he didn't feel the same way about her being a celebrity, even if she did look beautiful in the shimmery gowns she sometimes wore.

Margot shifted in her chair, and Zeke glanced over at her, feeling a sudden rush of heat. Or was it discomfort? He barely knew the difference anymore.

Either way, he broke the tension by changing the subject yet again. He said to Liam, "You're a really good swimmer. Who taught you to swim like that?"

"One of my old foster moms. She was a swim instructor. She gave lessons at her house. But the pool had a big fence around it so none of the little kids would fall in." The boy rocked in his seat. "Mom said that you like to surf. I've never tried it. But I want to someday."

"I started bodyboarding when I was around your age. That's easier than surfing at first." Zeke's dad used to take him to the beach. His mom rarely went along, unless they were on a private holiday in a secluded location, where they could avoid the public and the paparazzi. "I can teach you to bodyboard if you're interested. We can do it at my house." Because the invitation slipped out before he could run it by Margot, he added, "Your mom can be there, too, of course."

"That would be so much fun!" Liam turned to his

mother and implored her. "Can we go to his house and do that? Can we, please?"

She calmly replied, "Yes, but we'll have to arrange a time when it's convenient for all of us. We can't rush into it."

"Okay!" In spite of her levelheaded tone, her son was still excited. "Can I go back in the pool now? I want to pretend that I'm bodyboarding."

"Go ahead." She smiled, teasing him. "You can use the mermaid float."

"Very funny." He got up and grabbed the dolphin he'd been riding earlier. Then he changed his mind and went for Zeke's alligator.

While Liam was off doing his thing, Margot tucked her hair behind her ears, and Zeke noticed how enticing it looked, curling around her face. It was still damp from the pool.

"I'm sorry if I put you on the spot about the body-boarding lessons," he said. "I should've waited and talked to you about it before I said anything."

"It's okay. It'll be nice for him to learn a new sport." She fussed with her hair again. "He wasn't too thrilled about you coming over at first. He was worried about being bored. But you're probably the most exciting person he's ever met."

"It's been an exciting day. Lots of activity." More than Zeke had even bargained for.

Margot's phone signaled that she'd received a text, and she glanced at the notification. "Will you give me a second?" After she read the message, she said, "It was my assistant reminding me about a charity ball next Saturday that I agreed to attend. She's going to email me the tickets. It's a dinner and auction with an Old Hollywood theme, but I completely forgot about it." She heaved a sigh. "Between finalizing Liam's adoption and you coming back to town, I got sidetracked, I guess."

"You still have time to prepare for it." With her resources, she could pull it off. "You've always loved that sort of thing." And he'd always detested it, serving as yet another reminder of why they didn't belong together.

"I know, but now I have to rush to find someone to go with me. I can't ask Bailey because she's attending a writers' retreat that weekend. Maybe I'll call Jordan and see if he's available."

"Jordan?"

She nodded. "Jordan Nichols. You remember him, don't you?"

"The guy from your old acting workshops?" He didn't like the sound of that. He'd always suspected that Jordan had a thing for her back in the day. Not that he should concern himself with it now. Yet it still bugged him. "When's the last time you saw him?"

"He made a guest appearance on my show last season, and we've had coffee a few times since then. He just got cast in a new spy thriller."

Zeke didn't care if Jordan was going to be the next James Bond. Suddenly he was jealous of him again. "And now you're going to invite him on a fancy date?"

She shook her head. "It wouldn't be a date. He and I are just friends."

Feeling much too impulsive, he said, "If that's the case, then I can go with you as a friend."

"You? Mingling with my crowd?" She gaped at him. "You hate industry parties. You never attended anything with me when we were together, so why would you do it now?"

It was better than Jordan going with her. He didn't trust that dude not to turn it into a date. "What's the point of us being friends if we don't step out of our comfort zone?"

"Are you sure you're ready to step that far out of it?"

"I know how to behave in that scene. Some of the guests might even be Z-One clients."

"That's true." She appeared to be mulling it over. "But you've always made a point of staying in the background, and now you're offering to be front and center with me."

"I used to attend red carpets with my mom. Big major events. This can't be any worse than that."

"Okay. Fine. You can come with me," she reluctantly agreed. "But it'd better not turn into a disaster."

"Quit worrying. I already told you that I can handle it." Or he hoped that he could. If not, he was going to be trapped in one of the longest nights of his life.

* * *

Margot glanced around her bedroom, with its eclectic decor of chrome and glass and painted woods. How many times had she hooked up with Zeke here?

Too many, she thought.

Sometimes they never even made it to the bed. They would just go at it wherever they stood, bumping into the furniture and knocking things over. No finesse. Only urgency and lust.

She frowned at the vintage-inspired gowns her stylist had sent over, bunched together on a portable rolling rack. The ball was only four days away, and she was struggling with what to wear. At least Bailey was helping her decide. It was still weird, though, knowing that she was bringing Zeke.

Bailey reached for a sparkly green number loaded with sequins. "This color would look good on you."

"It's too flashy." Margot wasn't drawn to it, at least not for this occasion. "Do you think I'm making a mistake?"

"By not wearing something flashy?"

"No. By letting your brother escort me."

"That's tough to say. It could strengthen your friendship or it could backfire and seem like a date. Fine dining, drinking, dancing…"

Margot studied a purple dress with a plunging neckline. She definitely wasn't wearing that. "I never said that I was going to dance with him." She remembered how beautifully they'd glided across the floor together at their wedding reception, but that wasn't something she should be rehashing. Memories of their wedding always left her pained. She'd loved him so much back then, she'd thought they were going to be together forever.

Margot scowled at the dresses again. "Normally I enjoy doing this. But I just can't seem to concentrate today."

"I know how you feel. I have a lot on my plate, too. The day after I return from my retreat is Mom's surgery."

"It's nice that you agreed to help look after her."

"What was I thinking, letting her talk me into that?" Bailey shook her head, making her antenna-style ponytail swish. "I must be crazy."

"You are, but that's why I love you."

"I love you, too. But you need to get your rear in gear and choose a dress. At this rate, you'll be going in the nude."

"That's all I need, to be naked in front of your brother after ending my affair with him."

"That would be a bit of an issue. Maybe you should wear a really ugly gown to throw him off your scent. The yellow monstrosity with the feathers ought to do the trick."

Margot laughed. "I'll look like a bird."

"No kidding. I mean, seriously, did your stylist include that as a joke?" Bailey flapped her arms and made clucking sounds. "Instead of ballroom dances, you can do the funky chicken."

"I won't be dancing at all, remember?" Margot chose three gowns that held possibility, hanging them side by side. "Hopefully one of these will do." She proceeded to strip down and try on the first dress, a flirty silhouette with a snug bodice and full skirt.

"Do you need help with the zipper?" Bailey asked.

"No. I got it." It closed on the side, under her arm. But the dang thing was still too tight. She could barely breathe, and one thing she needed to do when she was around Zeke was breathe.

The second gown had too much fabric. It overwhelmed her, bunching in places it shouldn't.

And the third one…

"Now we're getting somewhere." Bailey approached her. "That looks amazing on you."

Margot stood in front of the cheval mirror, angling it to get a better view. The gold satin dress hugged her waist and flowed at the hemline, with one long, lean slit that showcased her legs. It was definitely flattering. "Hair up or down?" She held it up, then dropped it back down.

"I don't know. You'll have to work that out with your hair person. Who are you going to use on such short notice?"

"I already booked Martell Johnson. He's new, but he's good. He's going to do my makeup, too."

"Is he coming to the house?"

"Yes. I wanted to skip the salon."

"I'm always up for skipping the salon. God, I hate those gossipy places." Bailey stood behind her and met her eye in the mirror. "What about your jewelry and shoes and all that?"

"Maybe I can wear emerald earrings. I have a pair that dangle a bit. I also have gold pumps and a gold evening bag I can try, as long as the shades match."

"You'll figure it out." Bailey moved away from the mirror. "You always put yourself together so well. I wonder what type of outfit would be good for our high school reunion."

Margot shrugged. "Who cares? We're not going anyway."

"I know we agreed to skip it, but I've actually been thinking about going."

"Seriously?" Margot couldn't imagine a worse idea. It had been fifteen years since they'd graduated, since that particular hell had ended. They'd both been bullied something fierce in high school. The other kids picked on Bailey because she was the awkward daughter of a sex symbol, and they'd made fun of Margot because they thought the sassy character she'd played on TV was stupid. Prior to the cancellation of her show, she'd been tutored on set, and that didn't help her social skills, either. But Bailey had experienced even more trouble. She used to stutter when she got nervous. Sometimes she still did. "What made you change your mind?"

"I guess I want to prove to myself and everyone else that I've changed. That I'm stronger now than I was back then. But I have some time to think about it. The reunion is still four months away."

"It sounds daunting to me. But I understand where you're coming from, having something to prove." Margot had done her fair share of touting her strengths, of showing the world that she'd changed. But attending their reunion? "You're braver than I am."

"I guess we'll see. I haven't decided for sure." Bailey sat on the edge of the bed. "I wonder if Wade Butler will be there."

"Now, there's a blast from the past." Wade had been a fellow student, an oddly quiet computer nerd who'd gotten bullied, too. He rarely interacted with anyone, but he still came to Bailey's defense whenever he saw someone picking on her. "He was your hero."

Zeke's sister sighed. "I really liked him, despite how withdrawn he was. I think he liked me, too, but he never asked me out or did anything about it."

"It's probably just as well, with how things turned out for him back then." At the end of their senior year, Wade had gone to prison for hacking into the FBI and solving some of their cyber division crimes. But not before he'd bragged about it online under the white-hat alias he'd created.

"He's a big-time tech billionaire now."

"He is?" Margot hadn't been aware of his progression.

Bailey nodded. "I saw a feature on him in *En-*

trepreneur. He lives in San Francisco. It's probably dumb to think that he might go to the reunion."

"It's not dumb." To Margot, it made sense. "He might want to prove himself to the jerks who bullied him, too."

"I think he's already proven it. Even the FBI forgave him and started using him as a consultant. He's a philanthropist now, too. He does all sorts of good in the world. The article I read about him was impressive."

"Maybe so, but he's still an ex-con, and that might weigh on him. They arrested him at school, right after first period, hauling him away in handcuffs. That's not something he's likely to forget."

"Remember the long black coat he used to wear and those big scruffy combat boots? I always thought he seemed more like a goth guy than a computer nerd. He looks pretty stylish now, in the pictures I saw of him, anyway."

"I guess you'll find out how much he's changed if you attend the reunion and if he's there, too."

Bailey shrugged. "Maybe I'm fooling myself into thinking I should go. As much as I like to think that I've changed, I'm probably still a dork."

Margot smiled. "If you're still a dork, then so am I."

"A dork who's going to a ball with my brother."

"At least I'll be wearing a fabulous dress." Margot made light of her situation. But deep down, she was getting butterflies about seeing Zeke again. And in spite of her earlier claim, she actually wanted to dance with him.

Far closer than she should.

Zeke stood on Margot's porch landing, dressed in a black tux with a white limo waiting on the street. He'd yet to ring the bell. Instead, he asked himself what he was doing, taking her to a charity ball.

He'd been worried about her bringing another guy, he reminded himself. That was the only reason he'd jumped into this glitzy ordeal.

He finally rang the doorbell, not wanting to get caught too long on camera, just standing here. Margot's mom, June, answered it.

She flashed an appreciative smile. "Well, check you out. My daughter's security man. Or should I call you her BFF now?"

He laughed a little. "I think my sister would have something to say about that."

He'd always appreciated June and her pragmatic nature. She'd never told him off about the divorce, even if she didn't agree with his reasoning.

She invited him inside, and as soon as he entered the house, Liam came skidding around the corner, dressed in a pair of baggy pajamas and eating a cookie.

"Hey, Zeke! Guess what? Grandma baked these." He held up his half-eaten treat. "Do you want one? They're oatmeal raisin."

"No, thanks. I'll be having dinner at the party

I'm going to with your mom." He glanced around. "Where is she?" He didn't see Margot anywhere.

"She's in her room," the boy answered. "The guy who does her hair and makeup just left, so she's probably getting dressed now. Right, Grandma?" He turned toward June.

"That's right." She looked at Zeke and said, "You might as well have a seat and wait." She gestured to the living room.

"Sure thing." He adjusted his waistcoat and settled into a spot on the sofa.

Liam plopped down on the floor in front of him, and June took a wingback chair by a window. The kid ate more of his cookie, dropping crumbs onto the ornamental area rug. He was naturally messy, like Margot. Zeke suspected her bedroom was in full-blown disarray about now. She tended to toss things all over the place when she got ready to go out.

About five minutes later, she came sweeping down the staircase, like a goddess in gold. Zeke stood to watch her entrance. Liam and June hopped up, too.

Her gown shimmered in the light, hugging her long, lean body. Her hair tumbled across one shoulder in thick, shiny waves, reminiscent of Veronica Lake or Jessica Rabbit or whomever the style had been patterned after. Either way, it was hot. But elegant, too. Emeralds winked glamorously at her ears.

"You're the prettiest mom ever," Liam said, fussing excitedly over the woman who'd adopted him.

To Zeke, she was the prettiest damned ex-lover ever. He struggled to keep his eyes off her.

"You do look gorgeous," he said. "Really stunning."

"Thank you, both of you." She curtsied to her son, then met Zeke's gaze for a highly charged moment. "You look incredible, too."

He shrugged. By now, he was starting to feel like an anxious teenager on a fussy prom date with a girl who only wanted to be his friend.

June moved forward and said to her daughter, "You're an absolute vision. I love what Martell did with your hair and makeup."

"It fits the theme." Margot batted her fake lashes. "Theatrical eyes and full lips."

Lust-tinged lips, Zeke thought. Red-hot and passionate. But this wasn't the night for kissing them. "Are you ready to head out?" he asked. He wanted to get this show on the road. Or better yet, skip it altogether.

She nodded and hugged Liam goodbye, pulling him tight against her. She didn't seem concerned about him getting cookie crumbs on her dress. Luckily, he managed not to. Her gown remained as sleek and sexy as when she'd first glided down the stairs.

As soon as Zeke and Margot were outside, he took a cleansing breath. Yet it barely made a dent in his anxiety.

He walked her to the limo, and their driver opened the door so she could climb into the car.

Zeke followed her into the back seat, and once they were on their way, he closed the privacy panel and opened the moonroof. The ball was being held at a nearby hotel, so they didn't have far to go. But now that it was just the two of them, they both fell silent.

He searched for something to say, but all he could come up with was, "Do you want a drink?" The limo had a stocked bar.

She shook her head. "I'll have a cocktail when we get there."

"Yeah, me, too." Again, more silence. He glanced out the window. "Well, this is awkward. Us being so quiet."

"I can pick a fight if you think it'll help."

"Smart aleck." He relaxed a bit, losing interest in the window and turning back toward her. "What do you want to fight about?"

"Oh, I don't know. How about the way you were staring at me back at the house? It's a good thing my mom didn't catch you drooling over me."

He scoffed. "I wasn't drooling." He paused and shifted, the leather seat creaking below his butt. "Well, maybe I was a little. Your lipstick is sexy." He could still feel the heat of how kissable it made her look. "You smell good, too." He leaned closer, getting a sultry waft of her perfume; he detected a mixture of night-blooming jasmine mingled with cedar or cypress or something deliciously woodsy. He couldn't remember the brand, but she'd worn it in the past. He recognized the scent. "Will you dance with me tonight? We haven't danced together in a really long time."

She fidgeted with the slim gold chain on her glittery bag. "I already told myself that I wasn't going to. That it wasn't a good idea, even if I wanted to. But ask me again after I've had a cocktail or two."

"You need liquid courage to dance with an old friend?"

She met his gaze, staring straight at him. He stared back at her, too. If their affair hadn't ended, he would be sliding his hand along the slit in her dress, reaching up to cop a sweet feel of her panties. Then again, if this had been happening during their affair, she probably wouldn't even be wearing them.

"You're not an old friend," she said.

"A new one, then." He moved away from her, pulling back to modify his position. He'd already been leaning too close. "I'll do what you said and ask you to dance later." He would allow her to build up the courage she needed. He could probably use an alcohol-infused boost, too.

Or maybe he'd come to his senses and not dance with her at all.

Five

The ballroom shimmered in black and white with touches of red, the Old Hollywood theme evident in its decor. The nameplates on the tables were shaped like clapper boards, and brightly painted stars embellished the floors. Popcorn stands added bits of whimsy, surrounded by movie reel confetti. Champagne towers were everywhere. The guests milled around during the cocktail hour, checking out the memorabilia up for silent auction.

In this day and age most of the bigger auctions involved entering the bids on handheld digital devices, but this was being done the old-time way where bids were written on sheets of paper.

As Margot sipped her champagne, she tried not

to worry about the rest of the evening that was still to come. Dinner would be served by a waitstaff in vintage uniforms, and during dessert—something decadent, no doubt—the dance floor would open up with a live band playing music from the golden age of Hollywood.

She glanced over at Zeke. He was handling himself quite well, drinking scotch and water and chatting with Lenny Newberg, a prominent director who was at least twice his age.

When that conversation ended, Zeke returned to Margot's side, and they stood in front of a glass display containing a prop from a 1930s horror film.

"What's up with Lenny?" she asked.

"He's an old acquaintance of my mom's. He knew I was her son and asked me to give her his regards. He belonged to the same golf club as my dad, too. I gave him my contact information and reminded him that I was in security and that he could call Z-One if he ever needed me."

"It's good that you're networking."

"The potential for new clients is endless."

"Have you come across any of your current clients?"

"Yes, and they seemed surprised to see me in this capacity as a guest. But it stands to reason that they would be. Normally I'd be wearing an earpiece and standing in the back of the room, instead of attending the party with a drink in my hand."

"I'm glad you came with me."

"Are you?" he asked, a bit roughly.

"Yes, I am." She thought he was the most compelling man at the ball. But he was making her nervous, too, with how big and strong and serious he was.

He turned to study a colorful brooch once owned by Ann Sheridan. "Are you going to bid on anything?"

"I was actually thinking about bidding on that brooch. My mom always said that I reminded her of Ann Sheridan." She gestured to a cardboard cutout of the actress next to the display. "You can't tell by that photograph, but she was a redhead, too."

He made a curious expression. "I'm not familiar with her work. What types of roles did she play?"

"She could be sweet or sultry. A girl next door or a femme fatale."

Zeke released an audible breath, the chandelier above them casting a film noir glow. "You're definitely like that, too. Sometimes I think those qualities in you were my downfall."

Margot got a racy chill. He was gazing at her with memories of passions from the past in his eyes.

"I'll bid on the brooch for you," he said.

She shook her head. "You don't have to. I can do it myself."

"No, let me. Then if I win the bid, I can give you the brooch as a gift. And if I don't, then it'll just be one more uncertain thing about this night."

She blinked. "Uncertain?"

"I still don't know if you're going to dance with

me, or if I should even pursue it, regardless of how many drinks either of us have."

Her pulse pounded at her throat. "My champagne glass is still half-full. Or half-empty, depending on one's perspective." She didn't know which way she was leaning.

He wrote down a bid for the brooch. There didn't appear to be anything she could do to stop him, other than bid against him. But that would only create an unnecessary competition.

"I'll keep checking back before it closes and increase my bid if I have to," he said. "I'm going to try my damnedest to get it." He paused. "It's for a good cause."

Did he mean the charity? Or was *she* the cause he was referring to? Margot glanced away, struck by his impact on her. Trying to distract herself, she said, "Maybe I'll bid on some items for my mom."

Going up and down the aisles, she scoped out five different things. If she won them all, her mom would have a sizable bounty. After she placed the last bid, she and Zeke returned to the party.

They wandered around together, stopping to talk to other guests. Mostly, it was Margot who embarked on those conversations. Zeke had gone quiet. Would he ask her to dance later? Or would he let it go? She couldn't tell by his behavior.

As the cocktail hour came to a close, they proceeded to their table, but all she could think about was the uncertainty of that dance and how it would feel to have his body pressed against hers.

The meal was exceptional. Zeke chose the steak and seafood platter, and Margot went for the vegan option even though she wasn't vegan. He never knew what to expect from her. She kept him guessing.

Some of her castmates from *The Grown-up Years* were there, sitting at their table. By now, they'd gotten the gist that he and Margot had become friendly exes. But they didn't know that he still had the hots for her. As always, Zeke's desire for Margot ran rampant. He had to stop himself from staring at her while she ate.

She chatted with the female news anchor sitting on the other side of her. Mostly they talked about their children, showing off pictures from their phones. The topic was foreign to Zeke. He couldn't exactly chime in. He'd always been the big silent type, anyway. It sounded like a cliché, but it suited him, especially in his line of work.

Would Margot have been better off marrying another actor? And what about Zeke? What type of woman should he be with? When he'd fallen for Margot, she'd seemed perfect for him. But there was nothing perfect about the way it turned out. Even this ball didn't make sense. He shouldn't be here with her. He should've just let Jordan What's-His-Face take her.

By the time Zeke finished his dinner, he was

frowning. He excused himself to check on the brooch.

He wandered over to the auction area and saw that he needed to increase his bid. If he wasn't so pigheaded, he would let someone else win it. Yet he was determined to acquire it for Margot. The last piece of jewelry he'd given her was the diamond-studded wedding band he'd placed on her finger, which she no longer had cause to wear. So why should this bauble matter?

Because it represented her in a way that made him ache, he thought. Her innocence. Her wildness. Everything that made him crave her.

He cursed under his breath and raised his bid, almost as if he was raising the stakes on his feelings for her.

He returned to the table and resumed his seat next to Margot. She was indulging in the dessert that had just been served: a lavishly frosted black forest cake with cherry filling.

"This is delicious," she said.

"I can tell." He thought she looked downright orgasmic, going after another bite.

"Are you going to eat yours?" she asked.

"Maybe just a little." He sank his fork into his cake, and she watched him taste it.

Damn, it was good. Thick and gooey and bursting with flavor. He ate a bit more. He'd always had a sweet tooth that he struggled to contain. But he worked off the calories in the gym. Staying fit was part of his lifestyle.

A waiter came by, offering coffee, tea or port. Zeke and Margot both chose the wine. Soon after, the band took the stage and opened with, "I'll Never Smile Again," a song Frank Sinatra had crooned in his youth with the Tommy Dorsey Orchestra. Zeke's dad had been a Sinatra fan, so he'd heard it before.

As the tune continued, Zeke sipped his port, letting it warm him from the inside out. The next song was equally slow and melodic. He didn't recognize it, but he appreciated the soft sound.

People got up to dance, swaying to the old-fashioned beat. Was Margot waiting to see if he would make his move? Or would she prefer that he didn't? There was only one way to find out.

"Have you had enough liquid courage to dance with me?" he asked.

She hastily replied, "I never finished my champagne from before, and I've only had a few sips of this." She fingered the stem of her glass. "I'm not impaired."

"Neither am I." He was on his second unfinished drink of the night, too. "Do you plan on getting tipsy later?"

"Probably not. What about you?"

"I'd rather keep my wits about me." He stared longingly at her mouth. "But I think we should dance together, regardless. Then we won't have to keep obsessing about it."

"Maybe you're right." Her voice turned breathy. "But you can't kiss me when we go out there. A friend wouldn't kiss a friend."

"I never said anything about kissing you."

"No, but you look like you want to."

He quit staring at her mouth. "I'm not going to try anything. I'll be the kind of friend you need." Someone she could trust, someone who would keep his yearnings in check. "I won't take advantage of you."

"I won't do that to you, either. No flirting. No encouragement." She removed her napkin from her lap, folding it neatly beside her dessert plate. Was she giving herself time to calm her nerves, preparing to let him hold her?

He knew the feeling. But he stood and offered her a hand, escorting her onto the dance floor.

Margot swayed in Zeke's arms, lost in an attraction that she wished would go away. He'd promised that he wouldn't kiss her, and she believed him. But was she as trustworthy as he was? Would she stop herself from enticing him?

A part of her wanted to seduce him, to charm him back into bed. But she needed to respect her own boundaries.

She'd never danced to old songs like this before, and now that she was in the midst of it, she imagined that she and Zeke were being swept away to another era. Would life have been simpler for them then? Somehow, she doubted it. The same problems that existed between them now probably would've surfaced in those days, too. When it came to romance, the world was a complicated place.

She lifted her chin. Their faces were close enough to kiss, to do exactly what they'd agreed not to do.

Could he tell what she was thinking? Did he know how badly she wanted to taste him? Would it cause a scene if they kissed here? This wasn't a heavily publicized event, but it wasn't completely private, either. Photographs were permitted.

Margot leaned closer into him, making the dance more intimate. The only barrier between them was her shiny little evening bag, draped across her body and resting at her hip. Zeke had taught her to never leave her belongings unattended.

He met her gaze, and her imagination took flight. Was he still bewitched by her lipstick? She hadn't reapplied it, but the formula had staying power. She suspected that her lips were still a wild shade of red, much like the cherry filling in the dessert they'd eaten.

Everything they did together tonight seemed sexual, every second of every moment. Heaven help her, but she missed their affair. The erotic feeling of having him inside her.

She pulled back. "I think I need some air."

"Do you want to go outside for a bit?"

"Please." She was desperate to cut and run. But it was her own fault for wanting what she shouldn't have.

He led her to the courtyard attached to the ballroom, and they stood off by themselves. Although the temperature was mild, Margot felt a chill. Zeke removed his jacket and gave it to her, clearly aware of her shiver.

"Thank you." His jacket was big on her, but it made her feel safe. Which was weird, considering how threatened she was by her attraction to him.

"Are you okay now?" he asked.

"Yes." She cuffed the sleeves of his jacket, rolling them up several times, so she didn't look like a scarecrow. "It's pretty out there." On the other side of the courtyard was a garden surrounded by twinkling lights. "Lots of flowers."

He nodded. "From what I recall, carnations were always your favorite. Do you see any of those?"

"I can't tell from here." From her vantage point, all she could see were some tall leafy blooms. Larkspur, maybe. "But you're right about carnations being my favorite. They're not fancy or exotic. But they're hardy, and that's what I like about them."

"The garden at my mom's always reminds me of our wedding. That damned maze." He frowned into the night. "Sorry, I shouldn't have brought that up."

"It's all right. We can't pretend we don't have a past or that reminders don't come up. Being honest with each other is probably the only way to get comfortable with being friends."

"Then honestly, us dancing together was a mistake. It just made me miss our affair."

"I know. Me, too." She couldn't deny that she'd

had the same reaction. "But maybe in time, things like that won't matter anymore."

"I hope so." He quit frowning. "It's nice talking to you like this."

She was calmer now, too. "You know what makes it easier? That neither of us ever says that we miss being married. We only ever say that we miss the affair."

He tugged a hand through his hair. "The affair was less painful. But I did get a family-type feeling when I was in the pool with you and Liam. It almost seemed like you and I were still together and Liam was ours. But it wasn't as big a deal as it sounds. That feeling only lasted for a second."

She could do little more than stare at him. "But why would you even get a feeling like that?"

"I don't know. I think I was just caught up in the moment. But I'm not under any delusions about us being a family. We're divorced, Margot, and nothing is going to change that."

That was true. Their marriage was over, and she wasn't going to worry about him getting caught up in one little moment. "Thank you for telling me about your feelings in the pool. With the way we're opening up to each other, we might actually be on our way to becoming genuine friends."

A slight smile appeared on his face. "I really want our conversations to get easier."

"Me, too." She smiled back, grateful that they'd

come this far without imploding. "What happened with the brooch?"

"I increased my bid, but I should probably check on it again. The bidding is supposed to close at ten." He glanced at the Rolex on his wrist, the classic timepiece perfectly complementing his formal wear. "That only gives me about five more minutes. I can check on your stuff, too."

"Okay. But you don't have to increase my bids. I'll take my chances with what I offered."

He dashed off, and she stayed in the courtyard, gazing across the fence at the garden. It wasn't anywhere near as elaborate as the location where she and Zeke had gotten married. His mother had spent a fortune replicating the labyrinth of Versailles, and Margot had been thrilled when Eva had suggested using it for the ceremony. It had seemed so magical at the time, a storybook wedding for a dreamy bride. The honeymoon had been equally spectacular. They'd gone to Samoa, traveling throughout the islands, the tropical air caressing their naked bodies at night. But that wasn't something she should be thinking about. Even as dazzling as everything had been in the beginning, their life together hadn't been a fairy tale.

Zeke returned shortly. He approached her and said, "I won the brooch. You only nabbed one of your items. The autographed still from *Citizen Kane*."

"That'll make my mom happy. She loved that movie."

"They said that we can pick up our stuff before we leave tonight."

"When do you think we should go?"

"That's up to you. This is your scene, not mine."

She nodded. The ballroom was filled with her crowd. The people he knew were either Z-One clients or associates of his mother's. Not anyone he would typically socialize with. "Maybe we can stay for a bit longer." She wasn't ready to leave just yet. "I'm enjoying the night air."

"You don't mind standing, do you?" He glanced around. "All of the benches out here are taken."

"I'm fine. I like looking at the flowers." She noticed that other guests were strolling the garden path, carrying their after-dinner drinks with them. "It's soothing."

"This is going to sound like a stupid question, but did your wedding bouquet have carnations in it? I can't remember what it looked like."

She remembered, all too well. "It was pink carnations, white roses and baby's breath. Your boutonniere was a rose."

"I was so excited that day."

"Me, too. But things didn't turn out the way we planned." Far from it, she thought. "I still have our wedding album, though. I stored it in the garage."

"I'm surprised you didn't throw it away."

"I never toss things out. That's probably part of why you think I'm so messy. Me and my clutter."

"I shouldn't have criticized you for that." He reached out to skim her hand with his. "Did you keep anything else from that day?"

"I have everything." Her dress and veil, her bouquet, her engagement ring, her wedding band. She could've sold those, she supposed. The princess-cut diamond on the engagement ring was huge. "I'm a glutton for punishment."

"We both are or we wouldn't have started sleeping together. The ink on the divorce papers was barely dry, and there we were, fighting and fu—"

He didn't finish his statement, but she knew what word he was going to use. "We weren't thinking clearly then." Yet they'd hooked up whenever they could, keeping it going for three excruciating years.

He didn't respond. She turned silent, too. The breeze had picked up, making her even more attached to his jacket.

"Do you want to go for a walk in the garden?" he asked. "The pathways appear to be well lit."

"Sure. A walk would be nice."

They left the courtyard and entered the garden through an open gate, her stilettos echoing on the concrete. They didn't talk. They just followed the trail they were on, plants swirling around them.

Finally, they stopped near a weeping willow bursting with fairy lights and took a moment to admire it. With the way its branches draped, it looked downright haunting.

"When am I going to see you again after this?" Zeke asked, drawing her attention away from the eerie tree.

"You want to plan our next get-together?"

"Isn't that what friends do?"

"How about next Saturday? You could give Liam his first bodyboarding lesson." She knew how happy that would make her son. And if he was happy, so was she.

"That works for me." Zeke moved closer to her, making room for another couple headed toward them from the other direction.

Margot had to move closer to him, too, in order to let the other man and woman pass by. They all exchanged pleasantries. But now the walkway seemed too narrow.

One little misstep, and she could easily get locked in Zeke's arms. Her pulse jumped, an urgent desire washing over her. If only she could kiss him, just once, to curb the craving. Except that once would never be enough.

"Maybe we should head back now," she said.

He agreed, and they followed the other couple to the courtyard, keeping a polite distance behind them.

Once they were inside the ballroom, they headed over to the auctioneers to collect their goods, which had been placed in charity-themed gift bags for easy carrying. After that, Margot sought out the other cast members of her show to let them know she was leaving, even though she'd barely spent any time with them.

The limo ride was quiet. Zeke leaned back in his seat, and Margot took possession of the bags. They arrived at her house without incident, except for the turmoil in her mind. She was still thinking about the kiss that wasn't going to happen.

He walked her to the door, and she removed his jacket and returned it to him.

"Thanks for going with me," she said. "And thank you for the brooch."

"Sure. Anytime. I'll see you next week. I'll get Liam a board and a wetsuit, plus the other gear he needs. Just text me his height, weight and measurements."

"I will. Oh, and I'll pack a picnic lunch for the beach, if you don't mind peanut butter and banana sandwiches. That's what Liam will probably want."

"I'm not picky." He took a step back. "Night, Margot." He said her name softly.

"Bye." She unlocked the door and slipped inside, her heart beating way too fast. If this had been a date, they would've kissed for sure. But this wasn't a date. Or anything that warranted a kiss.

Six

Margot spent the next six days plagued with thoughts of Zeke, still struggling to get a handle on her attraction to him and fearing that it might never subside.

But on this sunny afternoon, she was keeping busy hanging out at Bailey's house. Zeke's sister stood on a tall, metal ladder in her woodsy yard, attaching a swing to one of her massive trees, and Margot remained below, looking up at her.

"I always wanted one of these when I was little," Bailey said, as she hoisted the rope over a sturdy branch. "But we already had a playground at our house with a swing set, so Mom refused to consider it. Do you think Liam will like it? I was hoping he could use it, too."

"I think he'll love it." Margot's son thrived on outdoor activities. "He already thinks your house is like something out of a *Swiss Family Robinson* movie."

"Has he ever read the book?"

"Not that I know of."

"I'll have to get him a copy." Bailey finished attaching the ropes and descended the ladder. "It looks pretty good, huh?" She moved the ladder out of the way.

"It's lovely. Very old-world charm." Margot was impressed. She never would've accomplished something like that on her own. She wasn't the handywoman type.

Bailey sat on the wooden seat to test it. "This is going to be fun." She pumped her feet and got the swing going, soaring higher and higher. "I wish I had a vine I could grab on to. Then I could be like Tarzan, swinging through the jungle."

Margot teased her. "Wasn't he your secret crush when we were growing up?"

"No, smarty. But there have been some hotties who've played him. I wouldn't mind having me some of that."

"I'll bet." Margot switched to a more serious subject. "How is Eva, by the way? How did the surgery go?" Bailey had spent the earlier part of the week on caregiver duty.

"Everything is fine. I think she appreciated having me there. Boy, she's a diva, though. She ran me ragged. I swear, I waited on her hand and foot. Her household staff is looking after her now, but they always do."

"How long is the healing process?"

"Six weeks, give or take. I hope this is her last procedure."

"I doubt it will be." Margot couldn't imagine Eva putting up with the ravages of time. "She's going to fight getting older for as long as she can."

"Not me." Bailey quit swinging. "I'm going to embrace every wrinkle or saggy boob I earn. But I guess it's different for my mom. She was the *It* Girl of her generation. Other women aspired to look like her. Her beauty is her identity."

"We all have something that we think gives us our identity. Mine is my acting. There was a time when I identified as being Zeke's wife, too."

"Yeah, until he put an end to that." His sister sighed. "So, what's happening with you two? How was the ball?"

"It went well. Or as well as could be expected. I messed up and danced with him, but I won't ever do that again. Even he thought it was mistake and was sorry that he'd suggested it. It was just too tempting for both of us. Too sexy, I guess. And that's the last thing we need."

"At least you both know your limitations."

"I'm seeing him again tomorrow. Liam and I are

going to his house so he can teach Liam to body-board."

Bailey cocked her head. "Why do you look worried about it? Are you afraid that Liam isn't ready to ride waves yet?"

"No, he's a great swimmer, and I think he'll make a great bodyboarder and surfer someday, too. It's Zeke who's got me rattled. Do you think I'm ever going to get over him? I mean, *really*, *really* get over him?"

"As in not wanting to sleep with him anymore? God, I hope so or you're going to drive me nuts about him, like you did when we were teenagers."

"Speaking of which, have you made a decision about our high school reunion yet? Because if you go, maybe I should go with you. It doesn't seem fair to let you tackle that on your own. Plus, it might be good for me to get over that part of my life, too." She needed to grow and change, especially now that she was back to obsessing about Zeke.

"That would be great. I'd love for you to go with me. But like I said before, it's not for a while, so there's no hurry for either of us to decide. There is something else I want to share with you that I'm really excited about. I'm going to launch a nonprofit that helps kids who are being bullied. I'm thinking it could be a hands-on organization, with events for the kids and their families."

"That's a wonderful idea. Just let me know if you need anything from me. I'd be glad to do what I can. But I wonder if you should contact Wade Butler about it. Maybe reach out to him on social media? The last time we talked, you told me that he was a philanthropist and a billionaire, so wouldn't it behoove you to have him in your corner? Considering how badly he used to get bullied, I think he would take an interest in it."

"Maybe so, but I haven't even created a business plan. I'm not ready to make any formal presentations. I'll just wait and see how things go, and if Wade shows up at the reunion, I can talk to him about it then."

"But you just said that you were still undecided if you were going. How can you talk to him if you're not even there? Besides, aren't you curious to get to know him and find out what he's like now?"

Bailey made a tight face. "I'm not launching this charity so I can reconnect with Wade. That's not what this is about."

"I'm sorry. You're right. I was jumping the gun." She didn't need to push Bailey into conversing with her old crush. Margot had enough man troubles of her own. With the way things were going, she would probably spend another restless night, steeped in ex-husband anxiety.

Bailey got up off the swing. "Do you want to have a go at this?"

"Sure." Margot could use the diversion. Anything, she thought, to help her quit stressing about Zeke.

* * *

Margot sat on the beach in a canopy chair, watching the bodyboarding lesson. Liam looked cute in his wetsuit and fins. He'd morphed into an Atlantean, after all. Or a hybrid or whatever half-humans would be called in Atlantis. She wasn't an expert on lost worlds.

But she was an expert on lost hearts. She sighed, thinking about herself and Zeke. They'd both taken a for-better-or-worse vow, but he hadn't held up his end of the bargain. He'd bailed when things had gotten too complicated for him. Yet here she was, letting him be part of her son's life.

Liam was already getting attached to Zeke. That much was obvious. But as time went on, would he start to think of Zeke as a father figure? And would Zeke take on that role without even realizing it? She hoped none of that happened. It wouldn't be good for any of them.

She gazed at her son, out there in the ocean. He had a big happy smile on his face, even when he struggled to catch a wave. Overall, he was doing pretty well. He'd gotten the paddling techniques down and had already learned to duck dive, even if he needed more practice to perfect it. Either way, he was a natural. He had a great instructor, too. Zeke was being patient and kind, educating Liam about the ocean and teaching him to respect it.

When the lesson ended, Liam rushed over to her,

running ahead of Zeke. "Did you see me?" he asked. "Were you watching?"

"Yes, I most definitely was, and you were amazing." She was proud of her boy. "But I figured you'd get the hang of it right away."

"Me and Zeke are going to store our wetsuits at his house, then we'll come back here to eat. I'm going to build a sandcastle, too, using the bucket and those little plastic shovels I brought. Oh, Mom, bodyboarding is so much fun. I wish we lived at the beach."

She wasn't about to respond to his last comment. Nor was she going to tell him that back in the day, she and Zeke had owned oceanfront property together.

Zeke walked up to her, carrying the bodyboard he'd been using. "Are you getting enough shade?" he asked.

"Yes, I'm fine." Along with the canopy chair, she was wearing a big floppy hat. "I'll have lunch waiting for you boys when you get back." She'd packed more than peanut butter and banana sandwiches. She'd also brought an assortment of fruit and a variety of snacks.

"I'm totally down for lunch." He stood in front of her, creating a whole other block of shade. "But, Margot?"

She adjusted her hat. "Yes?"

"I'm not a boy."

She blinked. "What?"

"You called both me and Liam boys."

She roamed her gaze over him, hoping that he didn't peel off his wetsuit in front of her. "It was a figure of speech." And now she could scarcely breathe.

He shrugged, smiled, tunneled a hand through his hair, slicking it away from his forehead. "I was just kidding around. You can call me whatever you want."

Except her husband, she thought. Or her lover. Or anything other than a friend. She glanced over at Liam. He'd already removed his wetsuit.

"Come on, Zeke," he said impatiently.

"Hold on, buddy. Give me a sec."

Zeke moved away from Margot to strip down, but she could still feel the effect he had on her. The emotion, the lust, the hurt of being divorced. With any luck, she would get herself back on track while he and Liam were gone.

She didn't turn around and watch them leave. Instead, she removed a bottle of water from the cooler and took a thirst-quenching swallow. After that, she spread out a blanket and unloaded the food, getting ready for "the boys" to return.

When they showed up, they were hungry as bears. Liam sat down and placed one sandwich, two bags of chips and three cookies in front of him. Zeke took two sandwiches, a shiny red apple and a mountain of crackers and cheese. Margot sampled a bit of everything, including the yogurt no one else touched.

"These are good," Zeke said about the sandwiches. "Filling."

"They're the best." Liam took another massive bite of his as he plowed through his lunch. Margot suspected that he was hurrying so he could rush off and build his sandcastle.

Within no time, he left the blanket to work on his project. He moved closer to the shore, where he had better access to the water. He didn't want any help. By now, he was content to be by himself.

Zeke and Margot remained where they were, and she studied him, mesmerized by how powerfully the sun glinted off his skin. He wasn't her first lover. She'd lost her virginity to someone she'd dated before she and Zeke had gotten together. If she'd known that she was going to marry Zeke someday, she might've waited and let him be her first. Then again, maybe it was better that he wasn't. She already had enough sexual connections to him.

"We're going to have to do this again soon, so I can give Liam more lessons," he said.

"There's plenty of time for him to learn."

"Yeah, but it's going to be harder to arrange our schedules once you and I go back to work."

"We'll figure it out." She tried to keep her voice light, steady. "But do me a favor, okay? Don't ever let that feeling come back."

He sent her a confused look. "What feeling?"

"What you told me about at the ball. That when

you were in the pool with me and Liam, it made you feel as if we were a family."

"I said that it *almost* made us seem that way." He frowned at the half-eaten apple on his lap. "And I thought we already settled that issue at the ball."

"We did. But you and Liam are getting so close."

"That doesn't mean I'm going to start having a bunch of family-type feelings. It was just a mixed-up emotion on that first day. I'm not losing sight of what my relationship with you or your son is."

She fidgeted with the yogurt spoon in her hand. "I just wanted to clear the air and mention it."

He snared her gaze. "Then is it clear now?"

"Yes." But there were other issues still floating around in her mind, like the sexual tension between them that wouldn't go away. But she wasn't going to bring that up.

They sat quietly, finishing their food. Neither of them started a new conversation as the uncomfortable silence stretched out between them.

Finally, she glanced in Liam's direction. "I'm going to check on how the castle is coming along."

She got up and walked away, leaving Zeke on the blanket. She ventured toward Liam and stopped when she reached him.

"That looks great," she said. So far, he'd created a single-story structure with a square roof and domed accents.

He glanced up from his handiwork. "Thanks. It's

not done yet, but I'm putting some shells around the moat to make it prettier."

"Yes, I see." She knelt down beside him. "Maybe you'll be an architect someday. You're certainly good at building things."

"Grandma says that, too." He wiped his hands on his trunks. "But I might want to be a writer."

"Like Bailey," she remarked.

"Uh-huh." He pushed his hair out of his eyes. "Do you think Zeke can come over tomorrow so I can show him a draft of the book me and Bailey are writing?"

After the discussion she'd just had with Zeke, she had no idea what his reaction to the invitation would be. But she wasn't going to deny Liam the chance to see him again. "He might have other plans. But you can ask him."

"Cool. Can I ask him now?"

She nodded, and Liam ran toward Zeke, leaving Margot and his castle behind.

Soon, both boy and man came over to where she was. Liam spoke first. "He says he can come if it's *for sure* all right with you."

"It is," Margot reassured Zeke, talking directly to him. She removed her hat, letting her hair fly around her face. For now, she just needed to stop worrying so much. Eventually Zeke would go back to work and start traveling again. He wouldn't be around much to see Liam later on, anyway. "It's totally fine."

"Then I'll be there for certain." Her ex stayed a cautious distance away from her. A moment later, he said to Liam, "That's a mighty fine sandcastle. After you're done, you can offer it to the sea as a gift for welcoming us today."

"Do you think there's mermaids and stuff like that out there?" Liam asked him.

"I'd like to think so." Zeke bent down to draw a mermaid in the wet sand at his feet. He gave the creature wavy hair, similar to Margot's, which was whipping wildly in the wind.

When he stood, he met her gaze, sending a sensual chill down her spine, the way he always did.

Zeke sat next to Liam on the sofa in Margot's living room, paging through Liam's manuscript. Margot was in the den, and Zeke assumed that she was purposely leaving them alone. Was she trying to prove that she'd made peace with him getting close to her son? Or was she merely trying to respect Liam's privacy and let him show off his writing by himself?

"At first I wasn't sure what kind of dog to make Nina," the boy said about the canine character he'd created. "But I chose an Irish setter because they're smart and affectionate, and they get along with kids and other animals. I wanted Nina to be like that. I did research on all kinds of breeds before I picked one. Bailey said that was important. She researches the stuff she writes."

"My sister has always been a stickler for detail. But when she was younger, she used to spend too much time alone. It was good when she and Margot became friends. They needed each other."

"I have a new friend at school. He might be my best friend someday. I make friends pretty easy, but I'm used to having to do that."

Zeke couldn't imagine being in foster care, going from home to home, adapting to different environments. Zeke's childhood hadn't been ideal, but it beat the heck out of Liam's. Up until the adoption, Margot's son had been at the mercy of strangers. "It's nice that you know how to make friends."

The kid smiled. "You're my friend now."

"Yes, I am." He thought Liam was an awesome little dude. Wise for his age, but tender at heart, too. Zeke glanced at the manuscript. "Are you going to do the illustrations for this?"

"Heck, no. Bailey is going to hire someone. But I get to tell them how I want them to draw Nina. Another reason I made her an Irish setter is because that breed has red hair."

"Like Margot's?" Zeke figured that was an easy call.

"And my birth mom's. Her name was Daisy."

Zeke was aware of who Daisy was. He had information about her in Liam's security file, along with a photograph that Margot had provided. But unlike Margot, Daisy wasn't a natural redhead. Her short choppy locks had been dyed. "Did Margot tell you about Daisy's hair?"

"No. She gave me a picture of her. I keep it in my room, but I can go get it." The kid gazed expectantly at him. "Do you want to see it?"

"Yes, I absolutely would." It was probably the same one that he had on file, but he didn't want to deprive Liam of the act of showing it to him.

While the exuberant eight-year-old headed for the staircase, running and skidding across the floor, Zeke remained on the sofa. Margot should've told him that she'd given Liam his birth mother's picture. From a security standpoint, things like that mattered. But Zeke would discuss it with Margot later.

Liam returned shortly, carrying an eight-by-ten of a pale, thin young woman with bright copper hair and soft brown eyes. It was definitely the same image.

The boy plopped back onto the sofa, scooting in tight. "This is her."

Zeke took the picture and said, "You have her smile. Her eyes, too. It's a nice combination."

"Thanks." Liam moved even closer. "Can I tell you a secret?"

"I suppose it depends on what it is."

"It's about my mom."

"Which one?"

"Margot."

Well, hell. "Yes, you can tell me. But if I think

it's something that you should share with her, I'm going to encourage you to tell her."

"All right." Liam squirmed a little. "Before she became my mom, I met her at a foster kids' charity thing. Lots of other celebrities were there, too."

"I know how you first met and how the adoption came to be."

"Oh, okay. But here's the secret part. I already liked Margot from her TV show before I met her. I even streamed her old show, the one where she was a kid in it. She was my favorite person on TV, and I used to imagine having a mom like her. But I never told her that I was one of her fans."

Zeke knit his brows. "Why not?"

"Because I don't want her to think that I only wanted her to be my mom because she's famous. She knows that I watch her show now, but she doesn't know that I've always been watching it."

"You should tell her. I think she would be flattered that you imagined having a mom like her, too. It might even be fate that brought you together."

"What is fate? I hear people say that all the time, but I don't know what it means."

"It's when something is meant to happen."

"Will you be there when I tell her?"

"If it'll be easier for you. It's important that she knows how you feel." Zeke's own feelings about Margot's celebrity didn't match Liam's, though. Their marriage had dissolved over the sequel of her show. Yet for Liam, seeing her on TV had factored into his dream of a perfect mom.

"I don't remember Daisy. But do you think that somehow I remembered the color of her hair? So that when I saw Margot on TV, I imagined her as my mom?"

"That's entirely possible. But the bond you have with Margot goes beyond that now."

"I love her a lot."

"And she loves you."

Liam leaned forward. "Should I talk to her now?"

"If you're ready, sure." Zeke placed Daisy's picture on the coffee table and they went to find Margot.

She was still in the den, sitting in a puffy gray armchair with her legs tucked under her, surrounded by floor-to-ceiling bookcases.

She glanced up from the iPad she'd been scrolling. "Are you done showing Zeke your book?" she asked Liam.

"Sort of…" the boy stammered, letting his nervousness show.

She frowned. "What's going on?" She turned to look at Zeke. Did she think that he was responsible for her son's sudden anxiety?

"There's something Liam needs to tell you," Zeke said. "A secret he's been keeping."

Now she seemed even more concerned. She got up and went over to Liam. "What is it, honey?"

He replied, "It's about your show." He went on

to explain, giving her the details, repeating what he'd told Zeke.

Tears filled Margot's eyes. "I think that's really sweet." She pulled Liam to her, hugging him. "I'm so glad I became the mom you always wanted." She gazed at Zeke and mouthed, *Thank you*, letting him know she appreciated him encouraging Liam to come clean.

Mother and child continued to embrace, and Zeke stood back, out of their way. Finally, when they separated, he said, "I should go home now." This tender scene was starting to become too much for him, making him feel like the outsider he was. But at least he wasn't getting that family feeling again. He sure as shit didn't need that, especially with the fuss Margot had made about it at the beach.

"Will you come back soon?" Liam asked. "Maybe some night this week? You can help me with my science project. I'm supposed to make a map of the solar system. I have to do a written report, too, and read it in front of the class."

"Sure, I'd be glad to help. I like astronomy."

"Cool." Liam gave Zeke a hasty hug goodbye.

After the boy left the room, Zeke asked Margot, "Will you walk me out? There's something I need to discuss with you."

She nodded, and they stepped onto the porch landing. "Is something wrong?" she asked. "You look like I did something I wasn't supposed to do."

In a sense, she had. "Liam showed me Daisy's

picture. But you should have told me that you gave it to him."

"Why does that matter? You already have a copy of it."

"It's a security issue, Margot. If he posts her picture online and announces that she's his birth mom, it could attract unwanted attention from someone from her past. Daisy lived a troubled life with some unsavory characters around her, and now her son has been adopted by a celebrity."

"Oh, my goodness. I should have considered that. But I don't allow Liam to go online without my supervision. I set parental controls on all of our devices."

"Maybe so, but that doesn't mean his friends' devices are secure. He could easily use someone else's. You're in the public eye. Being extra cautious comes with the territory. I'm not saying that he doesn't have a right to Daisy's picture. I'm just saying you should have told me ahead of time, so the team assigned to your security can monitor the situation."

"Thanks for letting me know. I won't do anything like that again without talking to you first."

"I just want to keep your son safe. And you, too."

"It's scary to think of the people out there who might take a nefarious interest in Liam. Not just someone from Daisy's past, but strangers, too."

"I'm not going to let anything happen to him. I'd die before I'd ever let anyone hurt either of you."

She caught her breath. "You don't need to die for us, Zeke."

He could've been dying already. Not in a literal sense. But suddenly, he was dying to touch her. To kiss her. To do more than keep her and Liam safe. She never failed to leave him in a state of bewilderment. She was gazing at him with confusion in her eyes, too. Between the two of them, their emotions were a mess. Sex had been so much easier than being hungry-for-each-other friends.

"What night should I come by?" he asked, trying to get himself back on track.

She only stared at him. "What?"

"To help Liam with his project."

"Oh, yes, of course. How about Tuesday? That'll give me time to prepare and get whatever art supplies he needs for the map. I still need to look over the guidelines his teacher sent home."

"Tuesday is fine." He would make himself available then.

But he had no idea what he was going to do about Margot, short of ending their friendship and never seeing her again. Only there was no way he could do that. He would miss her too much.

Seven

Margot busied herself in the kitchen, making zucchini bread from one of her mom's old recipes. But mostly, she was trying to keep her eyes off Zeke. He was at her house, sitting at the dining room table, helping Liam with his science project.

While Liam created a big colorful map of the solar system on poster board, Zeke did online research, printing information for the written report. Liam had checked out a library book from school that was pertinent to his subject, but he had to go through that himself. Margot wasn't going to allow him to slip by, letting someone else do all the work. Basically, his assignment was to write about why Pluto had been reclassified as a dwarf planet and what the criteria were for being a full-size planet. He was also supposed to include how Pluto got its name, and that's what Zeke was working on now.

"Was it because of the Disney dog?" Liam asked.

"Nope," Zeke replied with a bit of a chuckle. "It came from the Roman god of the underworld. In fact, it was an eleven-year old girl who suggested the name Pluto. She was the granddaughter of the man who discovered it."

"Really? Oh, wow. That's cool. Thanks for looking that up. It's fun having a research assistant."

Zeke chuckled again. "Is that what I am?"

"Yep." Liam grinned and went back to his drawing.

Clearly, her son adored Zeke. He wanted Margot's ex around as much as possible. And unfortunately, so did she. She was consumed with him, day and night, night and day. He was practically all she thought about.

"That bread smells good," Liam called out to her.

"It should be ready soon," she called back, hoping that was the case. She'd forgotten to set the timer, and now she couldn't remember when she'd put it in the oven. Being around Zeke was turning her brain to mush. Her body, too.

When she'd showered this morning, she'd fantasized about how they used to shower together. His mouth on her wet skin. His soapy hands. She'd relived every exhilarating memory, wishing that he was there with her. But she needed to break that cycle and stop having those types of thoughts.

Would it help if she got involved with someone else? If she took the plunge and started dating again?

She wasn't ready for a major relationship, but she could take it slow. She considered her options and how to go about it. Although there were exclusive dating sites designed for celebrities and other high-profile people, she didn't want to meet someone online. That was too nerve-racking.

What about someone she already knew? Should she call Jordan and invite him out? They were just friends for now, but he used to be interested in her. For all she knew, he still could be. It was worth a try.

She needed a diversion, and she trusted Jordan. He was a good guy. Besides, she'd already contemplated bringing him to the charity ball until Zeke had intervened.

She glanced across the kitchen and into the dining room to study Zeke. He looked up and caught her watching him.

Her entire body went warm, almost as if she was having hot flashes. She turned away and realized that she'd forgotten about the zucchini bread again. Heavens, could she be any more distracted? Annoyed with herself, she grabbed a couple of pot holders and opened the oven. She tested the bread with a toothpick. Thankfully, it wasn't overdone. If she'd neglected it any longer, it might've come out hard as a stone.

She removed the pan and set it on the stove top. She waited until it cooled a bit to slice it, slathered some with butter and brought two plates to the table.

"Thanks, Mom." Liam pushed his poster board out of the way and dived into the bread.

Zeke thanked her, as well. But she got the feeling that he would just as soon take a buttery bite out of her.

Neither of them had a handle on their lust. But at least she was going to try to do something about it, as soon as she possibly could.

Two days later, Margot and Bailey strolled along the trail near Bailey's house that overlooked the canyon. Although it was a common path for hikers and runners, it was quiet this morning. They walked at a leisurely pace, sipping coffee from travel mugs filled to the brim.

"I'm glad you're doing whatever you need to do to make your life easier," Bailey said.

"Thanks." Margot watched the sun rise over the hills. "Jordan seemed excited when I invited him to dinner, and it feels good to have gotten that part out of the way. Can you believe it? It'll be my first date since the divorce."

"Are you nervous?"

"No. But Jordan doesn't make me nervous the way Zeke does." He didn't make her body tingle or her heart pound, either. But she was still struggling with her hunger for Zeke. "I'm even nervous about telling Zeke that I'm going on a date."

Bailey clutched her coffee in both hands. "Why do you have to give him a heads-up? It's none of his business what you do."

"I know, but with as much time as we've been spending together, it seems only fair. I wouldn't feel comfortable seeing Jordan or anyone else without saying something to Zeke. I thought about calling him, but that's kind of chicken. I think I should do it in person."

"Really? Because I think telling him at all will just cause a big, nasty fight. Let's be realistic here. How would you feel if the tables were turned and it was Zeke who was planning on dating someone else?"

"Honestly, I'd be hurt and jealous. But we're only supposed to be friends, so it doesn't matter how it would make me feel." Margot glanced over at the prickly brush flanking the sides of the trail. "We can't keep having those erotic feelings for each other. It's causing too much stress."

Bailey heaved a sigh that drifted into the canyon. "If it was me, I'd go the chicken route and tell him over the phone."

"He's probably going to get mad no matter how I do it. But at least my conscience will be clear if I make the effort to see him in person. Besides, I think I'll be able to calm him down, and we'll be able to talk rationally. Now that we've become friends, we're learning to communicate."

"That's good. Because the last big blowup you two had triggered your affair."

"Don't I know it." Margot sipped her coffee, taking refuge in the caffeine. "But no matter how he reacts, it's going to be different this time. I'm never going to sleep with him again. That part of our relationship is over. I'm going to go see him tonight. But I'm just going to show up and take my chances that he'll be home. I think the element of surprise will be best. If I text him first, he might figure out that something's up. He's clever that way."

And on this uneasy occasion, Margot was determined to have the upper hand and be the person in charge.

At 7:00 p.m., Zeke's doorbell rang. He wasn't expecting company. In fact, he'd been getting ready to settle in and stream a movie. He was supposed to be on a break from work, but he'd spent most of the day on Zoom calls with his international team, reviewing their assignments.

He checked his security system and saw Margot on the screen. He answered the door, wondering why she was here.

She looked soft and breezy, wearing a casual spring dress and strappy sandals. But she seemed anxious, too, playing with the ends of her hair.

"Come in," he said, with concern.

She crossed the threshold into his condo, with its rugged furnishings and indigenous accents. Zeke's place reflected who he was, right down to the gourd pottery, bamboo window coverings and distressed wood floors.

"I'm sorry for barging in like this," she said. "But there's something I need to talk to you about."

He gestured for her to take a seat, and she headed for a chair and scooted to the edge of it.

Zeke stood near the bar. He should have offered her a glass of wine or a soda or whatever, but he was too impatient to hear what she had to say first. "What's going on?"

"I'm going out with Jordan on Saturday."

Damn it, he thought. He hadn't trusted that guy all along. "What the hell for?"

"I invited him to dinner. I decided it was time for me to start dating again, and I thought I'd start by going out with a friend and see where it leads."

He glared at her. "Where it leads?"

"Romantically. And please, stop looking at me as if I just said I was going to cheat on you. We aren't a couple anymore, and I didn't come here to fight with you."

"Don't lecture me on what we are or aren't. And don't play the pacifist, either. You're as good at fighting as I am."

"But that isn't my intention."

"Then what is?" His gut clenched, twisting and

turning into a colossal knot. "To flaunt another man in my face?"

"No. Absolutely not." She remained seated, clasping her hands on her lap. "With how deeply our friendship has been developing, I just thought I owed you the courtesy of telling you what's going on."

He didn't want to be her friend anymore, not if it meant getting hurt by her. "Why are you so interested in dating all of a sudden?"

She lifted her gaze to his. "Because I'm trying to shed my struggle over you. The lust you always make me feel."

"And that's supposed to make everything all right?" He didn't follow her reasoning. "You're battling feelings for me, so you go chasing after someone else? What does Jordan think about that?"

"I didn't tell him. The problem I'm having over you is personal. It isn't the sort of thing I can share with someone."

He scoffed. "I'll bet you told my sister."

"That's different." She zeroed in on the bar. "Do you think I could have a drink? My mouth is a little dry."

"Help yourself." He wanted her to get up, to come closer. He still stood near the bar. "Take whatever you want."

She glanced a bit shakily at him, as if his last statement was a double entendre. But she made her way to the bar and rattled around, searching for whatever he had available. She settled on pine-apple juice.

When she tried to return to her seat, he blocked her path, trapping her behind the bar.

"What are you doing?" she asked.

Being territorial, he thought. But he couldn't seem to help it. Even if Margot didn't belong to him, he still couldn't bear for her to be with someone else. "I'm not going to let you go out with that guy."

"You don't have the authority to stop me. Now step back and let me pass. I already told you that I didn't come here to battle with you."

Too bad, because he was trying to egg her on, to make her feel what he was feeling. The rage. The hunger. The lust she was trying to avoid. He didn't want to be the only one suffering. "What if I want to fight? What if I want to show you who's the boss?"

She came toward him. "I mean it, Zeke. Get out of my way so I can drink this and go home."

He refused to budge, glad that he was finally making her mad. "You can finish it where you are."

"Fine." She guzzled the juice and slammed the empty glass down. "Now you can move."

Fat chance of that. "Sorry, but I'm just dandy where I am." He flashed a cocky smile, pissing her off even more. She looked like she wanted to take a swing at him. But it would take a bulldozer for her to knock him down, and she knew it.

She hissed like a cat. "Screw you, you big jerk."

"Is that the best you got?" He mocked her, baiting her to call him every name in the book.

She narrowed her eyes. "I don't need this crap from you."

And he didn't need her coming to his house, telling him that she was interested in another man. As far as he was concerned, that made them even. By now, he should have let her pass. But instead, he shrugged and said, "It's not going to work, anyway."

"What isn't?"

He looked her straight in the eye. "You using Jordan to get over me."

"I'm not using anybody." She defended herself, a bit too vehemently. "That isn't what I'm doing."

"I'm just calling it like I see it. Nothing is going to cure you of me, except me."

She tossed her wild red hair over her shoulder. "If that's your way of trying to get me to sleep with you, you can go straight to hell."

"Fine. You win." He retreated, allowing her the freedom to get away from him. Only she didn't dash out the door. She remained where she was, as if a supernatural force was keeping her there. They stared uncomfortably at each other, a tense silence engulfing them. "Go," he said, reminding her that she could leave.

Her breath shuddered. "Do you really want me to?"

"No." He ached for her to stay, for her to touch

him, for him to touch her. "But it's your choice. I'm not your jailer."

"Yes, you are." Her voice hitched. "You've always controlled some part of me."

"Not purposely." He waited for her to make the first move, to come closer and let the moment explode. They were on the verge of another affair. He could feel it in the air, like storm clouds gathering in the sky.

She inched toward him. "Am I going to regret this when it's over? Am I going to hate myself for it? Or is this going to feel so good that I won't care?"

"I can't answer those questions for you." But he sure as hell hoped it was the latter. All he wanted was for her to pounce, for the rain to break free. He could barely breathe just thinking about it. He even counted the seconds in his mind, watching her, waiting.

One one-thousand, two one-thousand...

She rushed forward, slamming her body against his. He sought her mouth, and they kissed as if they might die if they didn't. She tasted like everything he'd been missing: his old lover, the woman he craved. He wrapped his arms around her, and she dug her nails into his T-shirt, trying to connect with his skin. They kissed some more, hot and desperately carnal.

When they came up for air, he said, "Take off your dress."

She did his bidding, letting the garment slide to the floor. "Now what should I do?"

"Nothing. I'll do the rest."

He lifted her up, setting her on top of the bar. She looked sexy as hell in her pink bra and blue panties, her sandals dangling from her feet. He carefully slipped off each shoe, pretending that he was going to take his time. But before she knew what hit her, he grabbed her panties and yanked them down. She gasped, and he suspected that her heart was beating like a runaway bride. She met his gaze, and he flung her underwear away, not caring where they landed. Her bra came off next.

He tugged her to the edge of the bar top and got down on his knees. He was tall enough to make this work, and he intended to have a nice, naughty feast.

He parted her with his fingers, and she moaned in excitement. She wanted this as badly as he did.

He knew her sexual preferences because they matched his own. She was the most compatible lover he'd ever had. The most responsive. Everything about her was positively sinful.

He buried his face between her legs, and she rocked against his mouth and made breathy sounds. He glanced up and saw that she was thumbing her own nipples, making them as hard as bullets. Was it any wonder that he couldn't get her out of his system? He could do this for the rest of his life and still want more. She was slick and wet, and he relished the taste of her.

She watched him through vivid eyes. So blue, he thought. So powerful. The lanterns above the bar were giving her an unearthly sheen. She reached out to touch him, putting her hand against his face. He pleasured her with every fiber of his sex-starved soul, and she arched her body, bending like a bow that was about to snap.

Or a woman who was about to come.

He grazed her thighs with his beard stubble and she shivered all the way to her toes. The sounds she made were wild now. She opened her legs as wide as she could, shuddering through her orgasm.

He stayed on his knees, absorbing her climax in the most intimate of ways. When it ended, he got to his feet, and she kissed him luxuriously on the mouth, melting all over him.

It was too late, Margot realized. She couldn't go back and undo it. She'd already let Zeke take her to delectable heights. They both were standing now, facing each other, her mind spinning, her heart pounding.

"Why can't I stay away from you?" she asked, still reeling from what he'd done to her.

"For the same reason I'm hooked on you. We're good together this way."

She knew exactly what he meant. Sex was their common ground, the thing that never seemed to fail them. She couldn't even begin to think about regret. She didn't want to hate herself for being with him, either.

She skimmed his cheek with her fingertips, fascinated by the rugged angles of his face. "It's your turn to get naked."

He agreed, and she helped divest him of his shirt, exposing his chest and abs, those to-die-for muscles. He peeled off his shorts. He was already half-hard. She rubbed him, making him fully erect.

He tipped his head back, and when she dropped to her knees, he nearly shuddered on the spot.

"Fair is fair," she said. She wanted to give him the same kind of raw pleasure that he'd bestowed upon her.

"You'll have to stop when I tell you to."

She looked up at him, this big, tough guy who stood before her. "I haven't even started yet, and you're already giving me orders." But she wasn't going to listen. Margot was determined to be her own woman, even if she was getting dangerously involved with him again.

She flicked her tongue against him, and he shifted his stance, watching her, getting ready for more. She took him in her mouth, and his stomach muscles jumped and flexed.

He tasted beautifully familiar, and she savored every solid inch. She took him deeper and deeper, as far as her throat would allow. He slid his hands into her hair, tangling it around his fingers, pulling and tugging.

"Damn you." He groaned, his excitement mounting.

Damn him, too, she thought. No doubt about it, he was her drug of choice, the needle in her arm, the habit she couldn't break.

They created a rhythm, with him moving inside her mouth. He kept watching her, and she increased the pace, her head bobbing back and forth. She could only imagine how deliciously dirty she looked to him, still naked and sticky from her own orgasm.

He was close. She knew the signs. She'd done this to him many times before.

"You better stop," he panted.

She kept at it, digging her nails into his butt, getting more aggressive with him. He cursed, his voice sounding parched. Sandpapery, she thought. He tried to make her stop again, but she refused. She enjoyed torturing him this way.

He gave up the fight and jerked forward, spilling into her. She let the feeling overtake her. Being the source of his pleasure nearly made her come again, too. She waited a few minutes, letting the moment swirl around both of them.

He helped her up off her knees, and she smiled.

"You look like the cat that ate the big bad canary," he said, his voice still crackly.

"Or the kitten that lapped up all the cream." She smiled again, teasing him, feeling full of herself. "I should get dressed and go now."

"What? No. We're not done yet. I still want you in my bed."

"You'll need time to be ready again."

"It won't take long." He reached for her. "We can cuddle or something in the meantime."

She was tempted, so damned tempted. Except that cuddling with him was about the worst thing she could do. They hadn't spooned since they were married.

Pulling back, she made an excuse. "My mom is watching Liam, and she's probably already expecting me back by now." She searched for her underwear. She found her bra on the floor, but she had no idea where her panties were. A second later, she located them on a nearby chair.

He climbed into his shorts, snapping the elastic against his waist. "You better cancel that date with Jordan or I'm seriously going to climb the walls."

"Do you actually think I would go out with him now?" She'd blown her entire plan of seeing someone else, of severing her sexual tie with Zeke. "I'm back to having an affair with you."

He bunched his T-shirt into a ball. "Then let's have dinner together on Saturday like you were going to do with him."

She hooked her bra and shimmied into her dress. "That isn't necessary."

"Then will you at least come over on Saturday?"

"Yes, I can do that." But she still needed to be careful, keeping herself from cuddling, from caring more than she should, from getting too attached to him.

Ever again.

Eight

On Saturday morning, while Liam was out shopping with her mom, Margot worked in her vegetable garden. This year, she'd planted tomatoes, bell peppers and a variety of herbs. She wasn't a master grower. It was more of a hobby.

About an hour later, she dusted herself off and relaxed on the patio, sipping iced tea garnished with mint. She'd learned the hard way that mint could spread and take over a garden, so she contained it in pots now.

As she poked around on her cell, scanning the latest news articles, her phone rang. Bailey's name appeared on the screen. Margot hesitated, apprehensive about answering the call. She hadn't told

Bailey about her latest rendezvous with Zeke. As far as Bailey knew, Margot was having dinner with Jordan tonight.

Problem was, if she let the call go to voice mail, Bailey would text. And if Margot ignored the texts, her BFF would worry. They never went more than a few days without checking in with each other.

Dang it.

She answered her phone with the customary "Hello?" as if she hadn't actually been stressing about it.

"Hey, you," Bailey said. "I just wanted to touch base and wish you luck on your date."

Should she lie and pretend the date was still on? No, she couldn't do that. She needed to be honest. "Thanks, but I canceled it. When I went to see Zeke to tell him about Jordan, it didn't exactly go as planned, and I—"

"Oh, my gawd." Bailey cut her off. "You slept with him."

Margot winced. "More or less." She forged ahead and added, "I'm seeing him again tonight."

"Are you serious?" Bailey sounded as if she wanted to shake her silly. "You're going back for more?"

"I know it sounds crazy, but I'm afraid that if I end it too soon, I'll never stop obsessing about him." She plucked the mint from her glass, sucking directly on the leaves. Just thinking about him stirred her blood.

"You shouldn't have told him about Jordan in

person." Bailey's voice came over the speaker, loud and clear. "If you'd done it over the phone, none of this would've happened."

"I know, but I'm not going to beat myself up over it. Being with Zeke is exciting. But it's not going to last forever. Eventually it'll be over for good."

"So, your hunger for him is just going to fizzle out? Poof, like magic, and it'll be gone? What if you start falling in love with him again?"

"That isn't going to happen. Believe me, I'm staying out of the danger zone." She'd already warned herself about getting attached, and she intended to tread carefully and heed her own advice. "I realize that things have changed a bit, and Zeke and I are friends now. But that doesn't mean I'm going to let myself be vulnerable to him. Our affair is just going to be about sex." Mind-numbing, body-blasting sex, she thought. "Just like it was before."

No, that wasn't completely true, she thought. Their affair wasn't just like before. Their friendship was creating a new bond. And to top it off, Zeke was becoming friends with Liam, too. He was good with her son. Nonetheless, she wasn't going to fall for Zeke again. She couldn't afford that type of pain. Nor would she put Liam through it. He didn't need to see her falling for her ex. Margot was determined to protect herself and her son.

Margot arrived at Zeke's place, but before she approached his door, she took a moment to gaze out at the ocean. She appreciated its moonlit mystery, the water rolling and foaming onto the shore, the aroma of salt and sea. She even imagined mermaids splashing in the waves.

"Do you want to go for a swim?" a disembodied male voice asked.

Startled by the intrusion, she spun around and spotted her lover sitting in a darkened corner of his courtyard.

She quickly said, "You scared me."

"Sorry." He stood and came toward her. "I was out here waiting for you, and when I saw you staring at the beach, I kept quiet and watched you. It made me feel like a voyeur."

She caught her breath. "Is voyeurism a new fetish of yours?"

"No. But it could be, if the subject I kept watching was you." He moved closer. "You didn't answer my question about swimming. I was thinking we could skinny-dip."

Her skin tingled beneath her clothes. "It's not a private beach. One of your neighbors could see us. Or record us."

He stood close enough to kiss her, without actually doing it. "Then it'll be your first nude scene."

He was teasing her, she thought, and using their conversation as foreplay. He had no intention of creating a public scandal with her.

He escorted her inside, and as soon as he closed the door, he kissed her for real. She moaned, clinging to him like a reed in the wind. In the chaos of the kiss, her purse slipped off her shoulder and onto the floor. He nearly stepped on it, but she didn't care. She ached to have him inside her, to have the roughest, rowdiest night of her life.

He scooped her up and carried her to his room, dropping her straight onto his oversize bed. He'd left it unmade, for this purpose, no doubt, and she landed on the mattress with a thud, the sheets bunching around her.

He crawled on top of her, pulling at her blouse, tugging at her boho skirt. Her shoes were trendy flats. He got rid of those in two seconds.

She wasn't able to divest him of his clothes, because she was pinned beneath him while he went after hers. Her itty-bitty panties aroused the beast in him. He nearly tore them in his attempt to yank them off. Once she was naked, he went down on her, lifting her legs onto his shoulders.

He used his tongue, and she writhed against him. This time oral sex was the appetizer, not the main course.

She reached back to grip the posts on the headboard, struggling to think beyond what he was doing to her. He worked his magic, and she tightened her grip on the posts, her vision blurring, her body feeling like it was splintering into fragments.

He made her come so fast, she barely knew what hit her.

He released her legs from his shoulders, and

she sprawled out like a sacrifice before him. She couldn't seem to keep her thighs together.

He peeled off his T-shirt and ditched his jeans. He wasn't wearing underwear, and his erection sprang free. She reached for him, and he kissed her, his mouth covering hers.

At some point, he pulled away to grab a condom from the nightstand and put it to good use. Then, as he braced himself above her, he said, "I want to make this last."

Was he referring to this specific encounter or the longevity of their actual affair? She didn't ask him to clarify. Eventually, it would all come to an end.

He entered her, and she lifted her hips to meet his generous thrusts. They kissed; they moaned; they rolled over the bed and knocked his pillows onto the floor. The room was softly lit, a glass-domed lamp providing a nighttime glow.

They kept changing positions, bending and shaping their bodies to fit. At some point, she landed on top, straddling his lap. She felt like a dancer, and he looked like an athlete. The strength of his arms, the definition in his legs, the ripple of muscle along his abs. Was it a six-pack? An eight-pack? She didn't know, but she rode him with lust and fury.

He reared up to kiss her, and soon he was on top again, thrusting with heat and passion. She moved with him, matching his rhythm.

Margot came first, bucking and convulsing and

clawing his back. He followed her, immersed in his own fiery pleasure and making primal sounds.

A few quiet minutes later, he got up to dispose of the condom, and she steadied her breathing.

When he returned, he stood beside the bed and stared at her. She leaned against the headboard and stared back at him.

"Are you hungry?" he asked, breaking the silence. "I can fix us a snack."

"Sure, why not?" She wouldn't mind having a little something. "Should I wait here or do you want to eat at the table?"

"You can wait here." He rummaged through his dresser, removed a pair of boxers and climbed into them.

After he left the room, she put her bra and panties back on, then returned the pillows to the bed and fluffed them. Zeke's bedroom was as striking as the rest of his condo, decorated in bold colors and aquatic artwork, showcasing big, bright paintings of the sea.

A short while later, he reappeared with a tray of food. She took one look at their snacks and sputtered into laughter. He'd made Dagwood sandwiches, the ingredients piled hilariously high between three slices of bread. In lieu of toothpicks, he'd used bamboo skewers to hold them together.

He grinned. "What can I say? I worked up an appetite."

"No kidding. But how am I supposed to eat that?

First of all, that's way too much food for me. And secondly, I don't take ginormous bites out of stuff the way you do."

"I know. But you normally pick everything apart, so I figured you'd dissect it, anyway, and just eat the parts you like."

She shrugged, deciding that he was right. She'd always been a fussy eater. "What kind of drinks are those?" She couldn't see the labels on the canned beverages he'd brought.

"Flavored water." He tossed her one.

She caught it, hoping it didn't explode when she opened it.

He handed her a plastic plate with a sandwich. She didn't bother asking what was in it. She would find out once she started taking it apart.

He sat across from her and opened his water.

"Can I have that one?" she asked.

"Why? They're the same flavor."

"It's carbonated, and mine got shaken up."

He switched cans with her. She sipped from the safe one, and he flipped the top on the questionable one. Only it was fine. No fizzy overload. He smiled and toasted her with it.

Smart aleck, she thought. She removed the skewer from her sandwich, got rid of the extra slice of bread and pulled some of the meat and cheese out. It was a messy business, and when she got avocado and mayo on her fingers, she licked it off. She glanced up and felt her cheeks go hot. Zeke was watching her.

Just as she reached for a napkin, he said, "I want our affair to be exclusive this time."

She hastily replied, "Neither of us was with anyone else last time."

"I know. But we left it open so that we could've been. And I don't want to take the chance of you dating someone else while you're with me. Not just Jordan. You already said that you weren't going to see him. But other guys, too."

"I'm not interested in anyone else." She had no desire for another man. "I need to get my fill of you first."

"I need to do that with you, too." He gave her a possessive look. "I guess that makes it official, then. Our affair is exclusive."

"Yes," she replied, and they both went quiet.

He lifted his sandwich and took a hearty bite, and she continued picking at hers. By the time he was almost done, she'd barely made a dent in hers. But she didn't want any more, anyway.

"Do you know what time it is?" she asked. She didn't see a clock in his room. "I told my mom that I'd be home by eleven."

He leaned over to retrieve his phone from the nightstand drawer. He glanced at the screen. "It's nine thirty-eight. Does your mom know that you're hanging out with me tonight?"

Margot shook her head. "I didn't want her to get suspicious of us spending too much time together, so I said that I was going out with some friends from my cycling class."

"Does Bailey know what we're up to again?"

She nodded. "I couldn't bring myself to lie to her. She isn't pleased about it, but I knew she wouldn't be."

"I don't care what she thinks. I just want to do wicked things with you." He roamed his gaze over her. "Do you want to have another go at it?"

Her pulse all but jumped. "There's no time. I need to make myself presentable before I leave, not go home looking like some unknown man ravished me."

"We can make it quick. Besides, I like ravishing you."

"I like it, too." Way too much, she thought. "But maybe I should get ready to go now, before you tempt me into taking chances I shouldn't take." Determined to keep her wits about her, she asked, "Will you get my purse for me? I left it in the entryway, and it has my makeup in it. I packed a wide-tooth comb for untangling my hair, too."

"Sounds like you came prepared. But are you sure I can't make you change your mind?"

"Please, Zeke, just get my purse and bring it into the bathroom. I really need to get ready to go."

"All right. But you can't blame me for trying." He headed for the door. "I'll be back in a flash."

She went into the master bath, and while he was

gone, she took inventory of his toiletries: his liquid soap, his cologne, the electric razor he used.

He returned with her purse and set it on the counter. But he didn't leave. He stood behind her, so they were both reflected in the mirror.

"What are you doing?" she asked.

"Admiring you." He moved closer. "You're beautiful, Margot. So damned beautiful."

Her hair was tousled, her mascara was smeared and her lipstick was gone. She looked like what she was: his reckless lover. And now she wanted him again.

"Is your offer still good to make it quick?" she asked, her voice going breathy, her common sense flying out the window.

"Hell, yes." He opened the medicine cabinet, showing her that he had a box of condoms in there.

"Then do it." She was still in her panties and bra, easily accessible to him. She focused on the mirror, eager to watch.

In the next wild instant, he pulled her panties past her hips. He shoved his boxers down, too, and snagged a condom, cursing when the wrapper took too long to open. Finally, he sheathed himself, and Margot pitched forward, getting ready for him. He thrust into her, and she gripped the sink and gazed ravenously at their reflections.

He moved in and out, nibbling on her neck, behaving like a stallion covering a mare. She turned on the water and splashed herself, getting him wet, too. But he didn't lose his stride. He maintained the pounding rhythm.

He took her so hard and fast the room began to spin. She could barely see straight, let alone watch their activity in the mirror anymore.

She came in a flurry, shaking while he spilled into her.

After he was done, he wrapped his arms around her, anchoring her so she didn't slump to the floor. She still needed to right her appearance and go home.

As if nothing had happened at all.

Zeke wasn't sure what was happening. The only thing he was certain of was an overwhelming need to see Margot again. But what did he expect? They were friends as well as lovers and that was a powerful combination. Besides, he liked her kid, too. So here he was on Monday evening, hanging out with her and Liam. He'd come to Hollywood tonight to meet with a prospective client, so he'd stopped by her place afterward, using the old "I was in the neighborhood" excuse to show up at her door.

She sat next to him on the sofa, and they formed Liam's captive audience. The boy was reading his Pluto report to them, the way he was going to have to do in front of his class. His project was due tomorrow.

After he finished rattling it off, his mom said,

"That was really good. But try it again, and slow down a bit. You were going a little too fast."

"Okay." He took a big, exaggerated breath and went through it one more time.

He enunciated the words he'd missed before, making everything sharper. He looked cute, too, his sandy-brown hair filled with static electricity from where he'd been rubbing the back of his head against the wall. He grinned when he was finished, and Zeke shot him a thumbs-up.

"That was perfect," Margot said. "I'm so proud of the work you've done on this. You wrote a really informative report, and the map you did is wonderful, too. But I think you better go take your bath and get ready for bed now."

Liam made a disgruntled face. "Can't I stay up a little longer?"

Margot shook her head. "No, sorry. It's a school night. Besides, you need to be refreshed for tomorrow."

"I guess." Liam gathered his papers. "Can Zeke tuck me in after my bath? I can come down and let him know when I'm ready."

"I think that would be okay." Margot turned to Zeke. "If it's all right with you."

"It's totally fine." He didn't mind tucking her son into bed. He imagined tucking her in, too, or just flat out spending the night with her. But he knew that wasn't possible. They might be having an affair, but it wasn't a relationship. They weren't heading back into something deeper. They both knew better than to get too wrapped up in each other. But for now, the sex felt damned good. He couldn't help but crave more time with her.

"I'll be back." Liam dashed upstairs, leaving the adults alone.

They stayed silent, until Margot moved closer to Zeke and asked, "Did you really have a meeting in the neighborhood?"

"Yes, I did. But it was also a good excuse to see you. Truthfully, I could've let Vick take the meeting." His partner had been available to do it. "But you know what would be fun? If you and I could arrange for a few days together. It would be great to go away somewhere, instead of me finding excuses to come here or you sneaking over to my place. But only if you're okay with leaving Liam with your mom. I wouldn't want you to do anything that would upset him."

"Liam loves being with my mom, and she adores being with him. She already watches him for me when I work or whenever I go out, so I don't see why it would upset him. He'll probably think it'll be fun with the way she indulges him." She hesitated. "But if you and I slip away, where would we go?"

"There's a remote house in the mountains that I've booked for some of my clients. It has a grotto and a lagoon-style pool, surrounded by forest. We could go skinny-dipping there, without having to worry about anyone seeing us."

She smiled. "You do have a one-track mind."

He smiled, too. "I just want to get naked with you, however I can." He searched her gaze. "So, will you talk to your mom about watching Liam?"

"Yes, but I'll need to come up with a story about where I'm going. I can't exactly say that I'm spending a few days with you. That's just a little too close for comfort." She sighed. "I guess I could say that I'm doing some spa days at a private resort."

"Whatever works. But let me check first to see what dates are available. I might have to pull some strings to make it happen sooner rather than later."

"All right. Just let me know. But we shouldn't keep talking about this. I don't want Liam to come back and overhear us."

They switched to another topic, and by the time her son showed up in his pjs, they were acting as casual as could be.

Zeke had never tucked a child into bed before, but he was going to give it his best effort.

He headed upstairs with Liam, doing his damnedest not to glance back at Margot or shoot her a hungry look. He couldn't wait for their clandestine getaway. He was going to try to arrange it as quickly as possible.

He cleared his mind and entered Liam's room, a big, bright space full of movie and sports posters, crates of toys, shelves of comic books, a snazzy entertainment center and a metal bunk bed.

Liam said, "I sleep on the bottom because it's bigger. The top is for when I have a friend stay over. There's also a trundle under here." He gestured to the area below the bottom bunk. "It's for guests, too."

"Have you had any friends stay over?"

"Not yet, but Mom said I can have pool parties and sleepovers in the summer." Liam crawled into the bottom bunk and pulled up the covers. "Did you have your own room when you were a kid?"

Zeke sat on the edge of the bed. "Yes, I did. Bailey and I grew up in a mansion in Beverly Hills, so there were lots of rooms. Our mother is an actress, and our dad was her agent."

"Really? Is your mom famous?"

Zeke nodded. "Very much so. Her name is Eva Mitchell. But you might not know who she is because her movies are from a long time ago." In the really early days, when she'd first started getting famous, she'd used her maiden name. But Zeke doubted that would make a difference to Liam.

The boy went quiet for minute, giving Zeke a baffled look. "I thought you and Bailey had different dads."

"We do. I told you that before."

"Yeah, but now you're making it sound like you have the same one. You just called the guy who was your mom's agent *our* dad."

"I'm sorry. I should have made that clear. My father died when I was a baby, and my mom married her agent, a man named Caine Mitchell. He adopted me and gave me his last name. Then they had Bailey about five years later."

"Oh, wow." Liam's eyes grew wide. "You're adopted, like me."

"I most surely am. I loved my adoptive dad. He was everything to me. I was really sad when he died."

"Does it make you sad that your first dad died, too?"

Zeke nodded. "I have lots of pictures of him. He was a movie stuntman, and he was even bigger and taller than I am. I got my features from him. He was Choctaw and Samoan." When he realized that Liam didn't have a clue what that meant, he explained, "The Choctaw are a Native American tribe, and Samoans are indigenous Polynesian people from the islands of Samoa. My dad was born there. It's a beautiful place. I've been visiting my grandfather there since I was a kid."

"That's nice," Liam said thoughtfully. "But are you ever going to get married again or have kids?"

"I don't know." The question threw him for a loop. How was he supposed to consider that while he was messing around with Margot?

"Do you think my mom will?"

"I have no idea." He didn't want to think about her acquiring a new husband. He'd already gotten jealous of that damned date she was supposed to have.

Liam sank his head deeper into his pillow. "I'd

like to have an adoptive dad someday if my mom ever gets married again. Brothers and sisters, too. I used to help with the younger kids in foster care."

"I bet you were really good at it." But this wasn't a conversation Zeke wanted to have. It was starting to make him tense. Or sad. Or some damned thing. "You should get some sleep now. Your mom isn't going to want you staying up half the night, talking to me. She was already worried about you being rested to give your report tomorrow."

"Yeah, she gets like that." Liam smiled up at him. "Thanks for tucking me in."

"You're welcome." He ruffled the boy's hair and got up to turn off the light and close the door.

Once Zeke was in the hallway, he shook away his feelings. He shouldn't be tense or sad or anything else. Margot's future and whatever it entailed was none of his concern. Nor was he going to dwell on it. But still, how would he handle it if their affair came to an abrupt end? Would he and Margot struggle to remain friends? Would her son get caught in the middle? Or would the boy be none the wiser?

Zeke didn't have a clue what to expect. But before he got too overwhelmed, he needed to get his emotions in check and take one cautious day at a time.

Nine

The house in the mountains was incredible. Not just the stunning glass-and-timber architecture, but the woodland that surrounded it: trees as far as the eye could see, wildflowers blooming on hilltops, a narrow creek flowing over branches and rocks. Nature, Margot thought, at its finest.

She inhaled the fragrant air while Zeke removed their bags from his SUV. Both of them had packed light since it would be a short stay.

"Are you ready for the grand tour?" he asked.

"Yes." She fell into step with him, and he unlocked the front door and ushered her inside. "How many times have you been here?" she asked.

"Just once, when I first checked it out to see if it

was suitable for my clients. I didn't stay here, but I learned all about it from the caretakers."

"It's amazing." The cream-and-gold living room showcased a magnificent view of the lagoon-style pool that Zeke had mentioned before. She walked over to the sliding glass doors to admire it. "It's so tropical." The yard overflowed with greenery.

"The pool is the focal point of the house." He joined her at the door. "It's accessible from the bed-rooms, too."

"That's good to know. Thanks for suggesting this place. I haven't been out of the city in ages."

"It's my pleasure." He took her hand. "Come on, I'll show you the kitchen. I asked the caretakers to stock it with ready-made meals, so we didn't have to worry about cooking for ourselves."

She smiled. "I guess it's safe to assume that or-dering out isn't exactly feasible."

He laughed a little. "This is definitely off the grid. You certainly wouldn't want to get stranded out here with someone who got on your nerves."

She squeezed his hand. "Then it's a good thing that you don't annoy me anymore."

"Same here." He leaned in to kiss her on the mouth, quickly, playfully.

Her pulse fluttered. She relished being kissed by him, even when it was just a brisk tease.

They entered the kitchen by way of a sunny breakfast nook.

She opened the fridge to poke around at the meals

that had been premade for them. "There's some gourmet food in here."

"I wanted this to be a glamorous trip. But outdoorsy, too. The best of both worlds."

"Then you succeeded." She closed the fridge. "Where do the caretakers go when guests stay here?"

"They have a cabin on the other side of the mountain. They're a husband and wife team."

As opposed to the divorced couple that she and Zeke were?

"Will you show me the bedrooms now?" she asked, struggling to clear her mind.

"The master is on this level. The other two are downstairs, in a fancy basement setting with additional living quarters."

"Then I'll just see the master for now." She could check out the rest later.

He retrieved their luggage from the entryway and took her to a room with a cherrywood decor. The bed sat on a sturdy platform, and across from it was a luxurious seating area and media center. There was a kitchenette stocked with nighttime snacks, too.

The adjoining bathroom had an old-fashioned tub and a modern shower, big enough for an orgy. Or two hungry exes, she thought, who couldn't seem to get enough of each other.

Zeke placed their bags on matching valet stands and asked, "Should we change into our swimsuits and check out the yard?"

"I brought three different bikinis. I wasn't sure if

I would need them, though. You kept talking about wanting to skinny-dip."

"I figured we would work our way up to that. By the way, there's a cave in the grotto where guests are encouraged to draw or paint or write on the walls. They keep art supplies down there for that purpose. The man who built this place is an artist and a bit of an eccentric, so that's where the graffiti idea came from. He used to live here, but he got too old and moved back to civilization. From what I've been told, he's fussy about who stays here. He prefers actors and artists and the like."

"Then I guess I fit right in." She waited a beat before she said, "Just so you know, I went back on birth control."

His eyes grew wide. "You did? When?"

"This week. I thought it would make things easier."

"You mean we don't have to use the condoms I brought? This is going to sound excessive, but I panicked about being in the middle of nowhere and shoved a full box of them into my bag."

She couldn't help but laugh. "One of the big boxes?"

He laughed, too. "A thirty count, I think." He turned serious. "But thanks for making the commitment that you did."

"Like I said, I thought it would make things easier." Nonetheless, she was uncomfortable that he'd referred to her choice as a commitment. She doubted that he meant it the way it sounded, but it still made her feel as if she was devoting herself to him somehow. Before she lingered over her anxiety, she said, "I'm going to put my swimsuit on now. But I'm going to change in the bathroom." She needed a moment of privacy to collect her scattered thoughts. She rummaged through her bag, nabbed the first bikini she saw and ducked into the bathroom. She hated that she still got nervous around him. After all these years, after being married and divorced, she should be calmer than this.

She removed her clothes and slipped on her bikini, a floral-print number that pushed up her breasts and barely covered her rear. Not that her skimpy attire mattered. By the end of the day, she would probably be naked, anyway.

She returned to the bedroom. Zeke had donned a pair of seafoam green board shorts. He looked like his usual self, tall and tanned and breathtakingly handsome.

"Damn," he said. "Check you out."

"What? This old thing?" She took a brave spin, modeling her suit. She'd bought it specifically for this trip.

He gazed unblinkingly at her. "You're a temptress."

"I try," she joked. "But should we go now?" She was eager to break his stare. He was still making her nervous.

He agreed, and they went outside. The yard was

even more magical up close. The rock formations around the pool had shiny pink stones embedded in them.

"What are those?" she asked.

"They're rose quartz. The owner I told you about believes in crystal energy. According to the caretakers, rose quartz is said to promote love." He frowned. "But people don't fall in love because of a stone."

To her, anything seemed possible at this oddly beautiful house. But in reality, she knew he was right. Those glittery pink stones weren't capable of casting spells. Or at least not on her or Zeke. Neither of them would be falling in love this weekend.

He pointed to a copse of sago palms and said, "There's a sauna through there and a row of outdoor showers." He motioned to a set of moss-covered stairs. "Along that ridge is a fire pit, and a little farther up is an impressive display of chainsaw carvings."

"There's so much to see." Almost more than she could take in. "This yard is certainly going to keep us busy."

"It's even crazier than the maze at my mom's house."

"A lot crazier." But she didn't want to think about the place where they'd gotten married. They'd already talked about it too many times before. She changed the subject. "What do you want to do first?"

"Let's swim and do some graffiti art in the grotto."

"I'm not a very good artist," she forewarned him.

He shrugged. "Neither am I."

"You're better than you think you are." She recalled a wild-haired mermaid he'd drawn in the sand at the beach that had looked pretty darned good.

"I'm all right. But it's just for fun, anyway. There's body paint we can experiment with, too."

"Really? And you're just mentioning that now?"

He flashed a sexy smile. "Are you game?"

She nodded, her heart picking up speed. "Where is the grotto, exactly?" The pool had all sorts of nooks and crannies. She couldn't begin to figure it out.

"It's supposed to be below the center waterfall."

"You lead the way, and I'll follow." She stood off to the side and watched him dive into the deep end.

He surfaced, treading water and waiting for her. She took a big breath and dived in, too. Once she came up for air, he turned toward their destination. Margot swam after him, feeling as if she was going to a place of no return, a land of the lost. When in actuality, it was just a man-made grotto—a cave, designed for play.

Once they passed under the waterfall, it was easy to find. The cave was bigger than she expected, with separate coves and connecting pathways. Some of the areas were dimly lit, others were bright and easy to navigate. She walked next to Zeke, exploring their surroundings.

The artwork was everywhere, on walls, floors

and ceilings. The people who'd come before them had expressed themselves in all sorts of wondrous ways. She noticed pictures in the styles of surrealism, impressionism and realism. Quite a bit of it mimicked prehistoric art, telling pictorial tales.

"This place is amazing," Zeke said.

Margot nodded. She liked the prehistoric imagery the best. As for the body art, there was a section of the cave set aside for that. It even had a shower, a mini waterfall of sorts, to remove the pigments from your skin before you returned to the pool.

"What sort of graffiti should we do?" she asked.

"How about if we just write our names? Then we don't have to worry about trying to compete with any of this."

"Okay, but only our first names. I don't want to reveal exactly who I am."

"Why?" He snared her gaze. "Are you afraid that someone might figure out that you had sex with me down here?"

Margot sucked in her breath. "We haven't done anything."

"Not yet. But it's only a matter of time." He used a black paint pen, writing ZEKE in big, bold letters.

She chose a lighter, more feminine script. As an afterthought, she drew happy faces on either side of her name, giving it a cute little flair.

Zeke raised his eyebrows. "Is that how good girls do graffiti?"

She shrugged. "I never claimed to be good."

"Sometimes you are, and sometimes you're not." He took her hand and led her to the body painting area. "And right now, you're going to be bad. We both are."

Mercy, she thought. Her pulse was already pounding in unspeakable places. She was excited to be bad.

The body painting kits came with a variety of brushes, water containers for cleaning the brushes and soft white cloths. Zeke decided to use his fingers. He wanted Margot naked, so he told her to remove her bikini. She undid the ties and let the top fall off. She peeled her bottoms down, slowly, giving him a show. She knew how much he enjoyed the smoothness of her skin. She'd always gotten full Brazilian waxes because it turned him on.

He dipped into the paint. He chose red for his first color. He followed the shape of her curves, applying the pigment in sleek lines. From there, he put flowers around her nipples, using purple and blue. He was careful not to smear the colors together. He rinsed his hands after each application and wiped them on a cloth. On her stomach, he painted green, leafy vines.

When he got on his knees and placed a pretty pink heart on her pubic area, it made her think about the rose quartz. Were those stones casting their spell, after all?

No, she thought. The heart he'd drawn translated to sex, not love. Lots and lots of sex.

He circled around back. She had no idea what he was doing, until he planted his hands on her bottom. He was making palm prints on her butt cheeks. Was that his way of being territorial, of marking her as his lover?

His final touch was a lightning bolt that traveled down her spine. She could feel the zigzag motion.

"What color is that?" she asked, trying to picture it.

"Silver, with specks of glitter." He came around to face her, looking into her eyes.

They kissed, but only for a second. She wasn't ready to get sidetracked. She wanted to paint him, too.

His big, broad chest made a strapping canvas. She used a brush and drew symbols that represented his love of the beach. She made wavy lines for water, a chevron for a seashell and a linear shape with stylized wings meant to look like a seagull flying in the distance. She wanted to add a dolphin, but she wasn't sure if she would get it right, so she did the basic outline of a fish.

She tugged his board shorts down, and he stepped out of them. She debated what to do next and decided on a sunburst around his navel, using orange, yellow and flecks of gold.

He looked like an ancient god come to life. If she'd been a better artist, she would've given him tribal tattoos. Zeke wasn't inked. Someday he would be. Tattoos were prevalent in both of his indigenous cultures, and as far as she knew, he was waiting for the right time in his life to honor those traditions.

"Are you done with me?" he asked.

"Not yet." She wrote a message in the V-shaped portion of his abdomen, right above his pubic region. An obscenity meant to arouse him.

He glanced down and read it, and she smiled at his reaction. It worked. He got instantly hard. He reached for her, and they kissed, rubbing their color-streaked bodies together.

He backed her toward the shower until they were standing beneath it. They kissed again, only longer this time, thriving on each other.

She rinsed away the artwork she'd created on him, making it disappear. Within no time, there were no symbols on his chest, no sunburst on his navel, no obscenities near his penis.

Zeke washed her, too. The colors streaked and ran, and she watched the pink heart dissolve into nothingness.

He nudged her closer to the wall, out of the spray of water. He bent his knees, grasped her hips and thrust into her. He moved at a thundering pace, making it seem as if there was no tomorrow. But maybe there wasn't. Maybe there was only today: this hour, this minute, this second.

He backed her into a corner to get more leverage. The cave wall was porous and bumpy, and Margot was pressed roughly against it. But she didn't care. She liked the jagged feeling. She wanted more.

And so did he. He lifted her off the ground, and she held tight, with her legs wrapped around his waist and her arms looped around his neck.

He didn't stop. He kept moving, stroking, pushing harder and deeper. He beckoned her to come. But what choice did she have? His manipulations sent shivers through her core.

Her orgasm erupted, and he watched her, his expression filled with intensity. When he shuddered and spilled into her, she felt his essence rush through her.

Like liquid fire, she thought.

Everything seemed so fast, so hot, so volcanic. She could barely catch her breath. He breathed heavily, too.

He lowered her legs to the ground, and she felt herself wobble. He steadied her, ever so gently, slowing the moment down. The fire was gone, but the sweetest of sparks remained.

An afterglow, she thought. A gentle sensation.

She put her head on his shoulder, and he stroked her water-drenched hair. This was a common feeling between lovers, she told herself, and nothing to worry about. The world wasn't going to explode if she cuddled in his arms.

Allowing herself the luxury of being tender with him, she closed her eyes and accepted it for what it was.

A romantic side of their affair.

Ten

In the evening, Zeke suggested a bottle of pinot grigio and a fruit and cheese platter, and now he and Margot were in the living room, eating and drinking.

As she spread a dollop of brie over a multigrain cracker, he thought about how much he was enjoying this trip and how soon it was going to end. Returning home to an empty condo was going to suck. He didn't like the idea of being alone anymore.

Would it get easier once he went back to work and started traveling again? He'd been spending most of his free time with Margot and maybe that wasn't such a good thing.

He scowled at his wine. Then why did it feel so

good to be with her? Not just the sexual stuff, but the moments in between, too?

"What's wrong?" she asked.

He glanced up. "Nothing."

She gazed at him from across the sofa. "But you're frowning."

Damn, he thought. He knew better than to be so transparent. "I got some crumbs in my wine." Dumb as it sounded, he couldn't think of another excuse.

"I didn't realize you were so picky about your pinot."

"I'm not, normally. But this is a great vintage." That part was true. It hailed from a family-owned winery famed for its whites. The process they used produced light, crisp flavors. "Do you want more?"

She extended her glass. "Thanks."

He refilled hers and topped his off, too. He set the bottle back on the coffee table and noticed an angry red mark on the back of Margot's shoulder, near the edge of the ribbed tank top she wore.

"How did you get hurt?" he asked.

She didn't crane her neck to see what he was talking about. Clearly, she knew the mark was there. "I think it happened when we were…"

Having sex in the cave? When he'd been pressing her against the wall? "I'm sorry. I didn't mean to…"

"It's not your fault."

"I should've been more careful. It's probably going to bruise."

She waved away his concern. "I'm fine. Besides, I've done worse to you with my nails."

"That's different." Or it felt different to him. "I'm supposed to be protecting you. It's my job to keep you safe."

"Our affair isn't part of your job, Zeke."

"I know, but I'm responsible for you while you're with me, and I should be taking better care of you."

"It's all right. Really, it is." She finished her crackers and brie and went after a strawberry. "Don't worry about it."

Don't worry? As if he could stop himself. He was still stressed about going home alone and being separated from her.

What the hell was wrong with him? The only other time he'd experienced these types of feelings was when he'd first fallen in love with her. He'd been desperate back then to spend every waking moment with her. In those days, he couldn't live without her. And what about these days? he asked himself. Was history repeating itself? Was he falling back in love?

Even if he was, it would never work. She was still a public figure, and he was still a guy who didn't want a celebrity wife. Just thinking about being in the center of that world made him panic. He'd spent his entire childhood in a fishbowl, and the last thing he needed was to spend his adulthood trapped in one. But that's what he'd be facing if he and Margot became a true-blue couple again. He had no business loving her. Or thinking that he *might* love her.

Struggling to breathe, he gazed out at the nighttime view of the pool. The lights were on outside, showcasing the yard.

"I'm going to go for another swim," he said. "But I hope you don't mind if I go alone." He needed to get a grip on his emotions, and he couldn't do that if she was with him.

"No, I don't mind. I'm nowhere near the swimmer you are. I'd rather stay inside, anyway. I'm pretty beat from earlier."

He came to his feet, ignoring the rest of his wine. He sure as hell wasn't going to drink it now. He needed to stay grounded. "I'll probably be out there awhile." For as long as it took, he thought, to get his head on straight.

"Then I'll see you in the bedroom later." She stood and smoothed her top. "But how about a kiss before you go?"

"Maybe just a quick one." He moved forward, closing the gap between them and intending to keep it simple. But as their lips met, she rocked against him, pulling him under her spell. She tasted light and crisp, full of flavor, like the pinot. He could've gotten drunk on every inch of her. He gripped her waist, holding her as if he might never let go.

Before he went too far, he ended the kiss, trying to knock some sense into himself. He didn't want to love her again. He didn't want to revisit all of that old pain.

He stepped back. "You don't have to wait up for me."

"I am a little tired, but I guess we'll see." She bit down on her bottom lip, sucking it between her teeth.

Now he wanted to kiss her again. But their chemistry wasn't the problem. It was his heart that was getting in the way. Still, he wished she didn't look so soft and sweet. He didn't need the distraction.

She gestured to their leftovers. "I should probably clean this up now, if we're both done."

"I definitely am." He hesitated. "Unless you need some help."

She smiled. "No, thanks. I've got it." She reached for the food platter and headed for the kitchen, leaving the wine for her next trip.

While she was gone, he went outside, stripped down to his boxers and dove straight into the pool, anxious to escape.

He surfaced, surrounded by waterfalls and rock formations. He ignored the rose quartz, refusing to give credence to the power it was supposed to possess. Whatever was happening to him wasn't because of those stones.

Zeke swam for what seemed like hours, taking long bold strokes, determined to feel better. Only his plan wasn't working. No matter how hard he tried, he couldn't seem to shake his anxiety. It didn't matter if he was a strong swimmer, or if he could cut through the water like a knife. He was still drowning, immersed in the fear of love.

* * *

Zeke awakened next to Margot, with the morning sun streaming into the room. She hadn't waited up for him last night. She'd been asleep when he'd gone to bed.

Was she awake now? Her back was to him, and all he could see was her tousled hair and the shape of her body, covered with a sheet.

He swept her hair off to one side and checked the mark on her shoulder. It was purple now. A definite bruise.

To go along with his tortured heart?

As frightening as his feelings were, Zeke wasn't able to deny them. He knew that he loved her. But what did he expect? If he'd loved her before, then he was certainly capable of loving her again.

"What are you doing?" she asked groggily, proving that she was awake.

"I'm just making sure you're okay." He kissed the spot where she was injured, touching his lips lightly to her skin, wishing she hadn't bewitched him.

She made a soft sound. "What time is it?"

"I have no idea." And he didn't want to move away from her to check. "You can go back to sleep if you're still tired."

"I think I'd rather stay awake." She rolled over to face him, smiling sweetly. "I'm sorry I crashed out last night."

"It's all right. I wasn't expecting you to stay up.

You had a long day yesterday. You don't handle the outdoors as well as I do."

"The curse of being a redhead. But at least I didn't get a sunburn." She adjusted the sheet, keeping it over her. "How long have you been up?"

"Just long enough to wake up beside you." He gazed into her eyes, nearly seeing a reflection of himself in them. She was the only woman he'd ever loved, who'd ever affected him this way. He reached out to skim her cheek. "You're always so pretty in the mornings."

"And you're always so intense, no matter what time of the day it is."

"I can't help it. It's just who I am. Besides, isn't that why you developed that old crush on me?"

She nodded. "Silly little me. I got caught up in the dark and broody."

"You're still caught up in it, still sleeping with me, still sharing a bed." He lowered the sheet until her naked body was exposed. His, too. They were both bare.

She reacted by pulling him closer, and they kissed long and deep. She rubbed against him, and all too soon he was braced above her. He couldn't make his feelings for her go away. Not this time. They were like a boomerang, always coming back. He damned her in his mind. But mostly he damned himself.

She parted her thighs, offering herself to him, and he slid inside. She was warm and wet and inviting, and he accepted what she gave him, struggling with whatever semblance of sanity he had left. Her hands were everywhere, all over his body, seeking whatever parts of him she could reach.

He increased the pace, moving fast and hard. She joined him, meeting his dominant rhythm. He lowered his head to lick one of her pointy, pink nipples. He licked the other one, too, then blew air across it, making her shiver.

She grabbed ahold of the sheet, twisting the fabric between her fingers. She looked wild and messy, free and passionate. But she'd always been an uninhibited lover.

She wrapped her legs around him, squeezing him with a viselike grip. Moans and groans filled the room, sounds of passion, hunger and heat. Her climax ignited his, and they came together, erupting feverishly.

He held her afterward, and she rested her head in the crook of his shoulder. Her hair tickled his chin, a silky sort of scratchiness, a sensation he remembered from when they were first married, back when snuggling with her made sense. He should let go of her. But he stayed where he was, keeping her in his embrace and wondering what came next.

Was he supposed to tell her that he loved her? Or dig a grave and bury his feelings in the dirt? Neither scenario appealed to him.

He glanced down at her. She'd barely moved since the sex had ended. She looked groggy again, her eyelids fluttering.

But it didn't matter if she drifted off. There was no hurry for them to get up, nowhere they had to be, nothing pressing they had to do. His only worry was the gut-clenching ache of being in love.

Her eyelids closed all the way. She was definitely falling back asleep. Cursing his weakness for her, he stayed awake, holding her unbearably close.

Later that day, Zeke's emotions remained on high alert. Nonetheless, he was trying to act casual, especially since Margot seemed so refreshed. At this point, they'd already lingered over lunch, and now they were going to go for a walk in the woods. But just as they were on the porch preparing to leave, her phone rang.

She checked the screen. "Will you give me a minute? I need to take this."

He nodded, and she headed down the steps without him. Clearly, it was a private matter. He stayed on the porch, but he could still see her, standing off by herself, engaged in conversation. Based on her expression, she'd just received some distressing news. Was it work related? Or was it personal? He couldn't begin to guess. Nor was he going to try.

Once her conversation ended, she returned to him and sat in one of the wooden chairs out front, as if she was still trying to digest the call.

He sat next to her. "What's going on?"

"It was about my show." Her voice quavered. "The network and the producers got into a dispute, and the network cancelled us. I never saw this coming. I thought for sure that our contract would be renewed and we'd be doing another season. And maybe more seasons after that. Our ratings were good. Everything seemed fine. But now I'm out of a job."

"I'm so sorry." He didn't know how to comfort her. Margot's association with *The Grown-up Years* had been a point of contention for him, the reason he'd divorced her, and now the series was gone. "Are you going to be okay, moneywise? I can loan you something if you need it."

She shook her head. "Thanks, but I have enough to get by for a while. I've been careful to make investments and put something away for a rainy day. But it just feels like I'm floating now, like my career might slip back into limbo."

He considered the timing. Was it a coincidence? Was it fate? Or something in between? "Maybe this is a sign."

She frowned. "Of what?"

"Of making a change in your life." And maybe going back in time and giving their relationship a second chance, he thought. Was that possible? Could it happen? Or was he grasping at straws? He couldn't be sure.

She stared him down. "Are you suggesting that I give up acting?"

"You did it once before."

"And it made me miserable."

"But it's different this time. You have Liam now. Maybe it would behoove you to consider a different line of work. Lots of former actors have created successful lives outside of the entertainment industry."

"I can't believe you're trying to talk me into throwing in the towel."

"Yeah, but you just said that your career might slip back into limbo, so what difference does it make?"

She blew out a breath. "I need encouragement, not my ex-husband spouting his old rhetoric."

"I'm not trying to start a fight." Arguing with her would only make everything more painful, and he was frazzled enough already. "I just…"

Her frowned deepened. "You just *what*?"

Should he say it? Should he admit that he loved her? That all of his old feelings had come back?

"Maybe we should take that walk," he said. Then he could decide if he should tell her. "It might do us both some good."

"Okay, but first I need to fix my hair. It keeps getting in my eyes." She removed a green scrunchie from her pocket and pulled her unruly mane into a high ponytail.

Zeke caught himself smiling. "Is that from the '90s?" She used to wear those when she was a kid. "Something you shoved away in a box somewhere?"

"No, smarty. They're back in style again. Some people are even donning them on the red carpet."

"Really? Damn. I need to pay closer attention to

the trends. You always looked cute in them, though." Her hair spilled out over the scrunchie. He leaned over in his chair to plant a quick kiss on her cheek.

She flinched. "What was that for?"

"It's just me letting you know that I like being around you." That was a lot easier than saying that he loved her.

"I like being around you, too, when you're not doling out advice about my career. But it's not your fault that my show ended. I wish they hadn't canceled it."

And he wished that he wasn't tied up in knots over her. He stood and reached for her hand, and she took it, hugging him when she got to her feet.

Without getting into another conversation, they exited the porch and entered the woods. The property was surrounded by ponderosa pines, rugged trees with a sweet smell. The trails were wide enough for them to walk side by side, the ground covered with twigs and fallen leaves.

They took an elevated path and headed higher into the hills. As squirrels scurried through the trees and a red-tailed hawk soared above them, Zeke glanced over at Margot. She plucked a long-stemmed bloom from a tall flowering plant and worked it into her ponytail, adding a spot of yellow.

When they reached a ridge that spread into a flat plane, they stopped to appreciate the view.

"This is beautiful," she said. "I'd love to bring Liam up here. But I'd have to rent a cabin or something. The house where you and I are staying doesn't seem geared for someone his age."

"I agree. It's more of an adult sanctuary, for artists and lovers and whatnot. But if you want me to ask the caretakers if they know of a kid-friendly cabin in this area, I'd be glad to check on that."

"Thanks. That would be nice. I don't know if Liam has ever even been to the mountains. There's still so much I'm learning about my son. He likes to chat at night, before bed, so that's when I seem to get to know him best."

"He was talkative on the night I tucked him in. He asked a lot of questions, too."

Curiosity lit up her eyes. "What kinds of questions?"

Zeke winced a little. "He asked me if I was ever going to get married again or have kids. He asked me the same thing about you."

She blinked. "He did?"

"He's hoping that you'll get married again someday. He expressed an interest in having an adoptive father and some brothers and sisters."

"Oh, my goodness. I had no idea that he was having those kinds of thoughts." She furrowed her brow. "As attached as Liam is to you, I was worried that he might start thinking of you as a father figure." She leaned forward. "He didn't mention you becoming his dad, did he?"

"No. He just talked about you marrying someone else. And that was a bit hard for me to take. I know we're divorced, but I never really counted on you having a new husband."

She sighed. "I'm not ready for anything like that anyway. I'm in the midst of the affair with you, and I just lost my job. Things are complicated for me right now."

"For me, too. I was okay when we first got here, but then last night, I started getting jumbled. That's why I went for a swim and why I needed to be alone."

She fussed with the flower in her hair. "What are you talking about? You're not making yourself clear."

He studied her, summoning the strength to tell her the rest of it. "I didn't mean to get this close to you. It was only supposed to be sex. And friendship." He couldn't discount that part. "But for me, it's turning into more." He paused, felt his pulse spike. "I love you, Margot. I fell back in love with you. But truthfully, I don't have a clue what I'm supposed to do about it."

Eleven

Margot couldn't speak. She needed a moment to keep her knees from buckling, to stop her hands from quaking.

Zeke loved her?

A fear rose inside her, a panic that she was in danger of loving him, too. Just hearing him say it, just knowing that he felt that way created a tunnel to the past and all the years that she'd loved him.

She met his gaze. He was looking at her, watching her.

She finally summoned the courage to speak. "I understand that you're conflicted," she said, struggling to steady her voice. "But what prompted you to tell me how you feel? It seems odd that you're mentioning it on the same day I lost my job."

He shook his head. "I didn't know your show was going to be canceled."

"But you never wanted me to be part of it. You never wanted an actress for a wife."

"Yes, and why would I? I spent my youth living in the chaos of my mother's fame—the never-ending paparazzi, the invasion of my family's privacy, strangers stalking us, tracking down our phone numbers, going through our trash."

"I'm aware of all that." He'd drilled it into her since the beginning. She'd seen firsthand how Eva's celebrity had affected Bailey, too. "I'm not naive about how difficult it was for you. But I had a right to pursue my dreams and goals."

"I wasn't trying to take your happiness away from you. But I couldn't spend my days worrying that your star was going to rise or that you'd become as famous as my mother someday."

"You shouldn't love me. It's not good for you. It's not good for me, either."

"I know, but I can't help how I feel. If things were different, I'd ask you to marry me again, to start over, to have the opportunities we missed. But nothing has changed, and it still hurts as badly as it did before."

His admission made her ache, and so did the tortured way he was looking at her. She wanted to touch him, to connect with his pain somehow. But she kept her hands at her sides.

"I'm afraid of loving you," she said. "Of letting myself stumble back down that path. But even if I loved you, I wouldn't give up my career or stop being who I am. That would destroy me."

"That's what makes it so hard. We already went through this in the past, and it made us hate each other."

"We don't have to hate each other now." She inched closer to him. "We can stay friends."

"What about our affair?" He moved closer, too. "Do you want to keep sleeping with me?"

She shivered, goose bumps covering her arms. Continuing to be intimate with him now would only create more pain and suffering. Yet she foolishly replied, "Maybe we can keep it going."

He shifted his stance, leaves crunching beneath his feet. "For how long?"

"I don't know." Margot fought the heat building inside her. She was playing with fire, and sooner or later, she was bound to get torched. "But I can't bear to give you up just yet."

"I'm not ready to let go, either. But damn it, I should be." He glanced up at the sky. Was he searching for divine intervention, for something or someone to set him straight?

The only thing she saw were clouds shielding the sun. "We're both mixed-up."

"Yeah, we are. But I really want to kiss you right now."

"Just kiss me?" She wanted to have full-blown sex, even if it was a dangerous thing to do. She was conflicted, from her heart to her soul, but she couldn't seem to control her perilous urges. "I think we should do more."

Zeke reacted cautiously. "Are you sure this is the time and place?"

She glanced around. "Here in the mountains, among the flowers? This seems like a perfect time and place."

He leaned toward her. "Then who am I to disagree?"

Grateful for his acquiescence, she tugged him to the ground, and they kissed, over and over, wrapped in pain and fear and lust. A restless combination. A whirlwind of emotions. Already, her head spun with it.

She moved quickly, stripping off her boots and jeans and panties. She was wearing a tunic top that fit like a minidress, which she left on.

He shoved his jeans and boxers down, and she straddled his lap. There was no one around to see. They were alone on a hilltop in the middle of nowhere.

He was hard and ready. She was ready, too. So damned eager to be with him. She impaled herself, her breath hitching on a moan.

"If only..." he whispered.

She knew exactly what he meant. If only they could build a life together, if only their differences wouldn't get in the way. But she didn't want to talk about that. She just wanted to focus on the sex. Yet as she moved up and down, rocking her body and creating a sinuous rhythm, she realized that she loved him, just as he loved her.

But it didn't matter if she shared his feelings. It didn't change who they were. She wasn't going to marry him again. She wasn't even going to keep sleeping with him. This had to be their last day as lovers, the end of their affair. It was different now that love was part of the mix. In the long run, it would only cause them pain. They were two people who didn't belong together.

She rode him with the passion that clamored inside her, that made her scratch her fingers into the dirt, getting little pebbles under her nails. Tomorrow she would tell him that it was over, that she couldn't do this anymore.

They were going home tomorrow, anyway. This trip was almost done. But for now, she just needed to lose herself in the hunger and make both of them come, as hard and fast and desperately as she could.

The following morning, Margot woke up late and discovered she was alone. Zeke wasn't next to her in bed, but she didn't ponder his whereabouts. Instead, she packed her bag, preparing to go home. Of course, she had to steel her emotions, too, and figure out exactly what she was going to say to him.

Should she admit that she loved him? Or just state her case about ending their affair? She decided that it was only fair to tell him everything. It was strange, loving him again. But maybe she'd never really stopped. Maybe she'd been repressing it all these years, claiming not to care when she actually did. But did it matter? Love wasn't the answer to their problems. There was no future for them, other than being friends. They'd both gone too far, and now she had to step back and hope for the best.

After she bathed and got dressed, she wandered through the house, looking for him, anxious to get her feelings off her chest. She didn't find him, but she discovered that he'd made a pot of coffee. She poured herself a cup, then diluted it with hot water. Zeke always made it too strong for her. She added her usual sugar and milk, still wondering where he was.

She could text him, assuming that he had his phone on him. But instead, she went outside to look for him by the pool.

Sure enough, he was there. He sat in a patio chair, in a faraway corner of the yard, gazing out at the water. He looked sullen but sexy, dressed in a plain white T-shirt, holey jeans and black sneakers.

Margot approached him, and he glanced up. She was going to miss being with him. Even now, she wanted to lure him back to bed and give their affair one more day.

"Join me?" he asked, interrupting her thoughts.

When she didn't respond, he gestured to the empty chair next to him. Fraught with nerves, she took the seat and put her coffee on a side table. One more day wasn't going to make a difference.

"I'm sorry I disappeared," he said. "I couldn't stay cooped up inside."

She merely nodded. "How long have you been out here?"

"Since daybreak. I watched the sun come up."

"Have you eaten?" It was a mundane question, but she couldn't think of what else to say.

"I had some toast and jam. What about you?"

"Just the coffee so far. I'm not really hungry." But enough of the small talk, she thought. She needed to broach the truth. "Zeke?"

His gaze connected with hers. "Yes?"

"What happened to you happened to me, too. The love thing," she clarified, forcing herself to stay strong.

"Damn." He released a rough, tremulous breath. "Really?"

She nodded. "But I think it's been going on for a while. It seems feasible that I never really stopped loving you, only I didn't realize it or own up to it until now."

He leaned forward in his chair. "Maybe that's what's been going on with me, too."

"Maybe. But love isn't going to save us. Our affair has to end for good this time. What's the point of us sleeping together when it will only hurt worse later?"

He frowned, his eyes dark and hooded beneath his brows. "I don't want to keep hurting, any more than you do. But I still wish we could be together for real. Can't you reconsider your job situation?"

"And give up acting just because my show ended? That didn't work the first time, and it's not going to work now."

"But where are you going to go from here? Most of your career has been centered around playing the same character."

"I know. And it's scary to think that I'll never play her again. But maybe losing my job was a blessing in disguise. It might work in my favor to try something new." She considered her options. "I always wanted to transition into film, and this could be my chance to get cast in a breakout role."

"And break free of me while you're doing it? God, I feel like I'm getting divorced all over again."

"Me, too." She ached just remembering it. "But we're being civil to each other. Last time, we fought like feral cats and rabid dogs."

He sent her a sad smile. "We weren't friends then like we are now. So that's saying something, at least." He glanced toward the hills. "When we get back to the city, I'm going to book a flight out of LA."

She started. "And go where?"

"To Samoa. I think I need to spend some quiet time with my grandfather. He's always been good for what ails me."

She had incredible memories of Samoa from their honeymoon. The dreamlike beaches, the rainforests, the romance of being a new bride. Images she struggled to grasp now. "Will you give your grandfather my regards?"

"Of course." Zeke stood, coming to his towering height. "I should go throw my things together."

"I already packed, so I'll just stay here and finish my coffee." She'd barely touched it. "I'm sorry for the way things turned out."

"So am I. But maybe we shouldn't have risked having another affair to begin with." He started to walk away, but then he turned back to look at her. "I'm probably always going to love you. But man, it's awful, loving someone I can't have."

She battled the urge to cry. "It's the same for me." Loving someone who couldn't handle her career choice, who couldn't be the lifelong partner she needed. Zeke would always be the husband she'd loved and lost.

When Margot got home from the mountains, she found out that Liam was sick.

Was this her fault for going away? For lying to her mom about where she was? For trusting that Liam would be okay without her?

In the midst of her guilt, she asked her mom, "Why didn't you call and tell me that he wasn't feeling well? I would have come back right away."

"He just started feeling ill today. But I think it's just a cold. He doesn't have a fever or a sore throat or anything alarming. His nose is stuffed up, so I gave him a decongestant and told him to rest."

Margot was still worried. This was her first experience with Liam getting sick. "Is he asleep?"

"I doubt it. When I checked on him, he was sitting up in bed, searching for something to stream."

"I need to check on him, too." Margot dashed up to his room. His door was ajar, so she peeked in and saw him leaning against a bunch of pillows and watching TV.

She knocked to let him know she was entering his space. As soon as he caught sight of her, a big grin spread across his face.

"Hi, Mom!" He put the screen on pause.

"Hi, baby." She sat on the edge of his bed and smoothed his quilt. "Grandma says you have a cold."

"Yeah. But I just started watching these funny old cartoons. There's this wolf that keeps chasing this really fast bird that beeps like a car. But the wolf never catches him."

She smiled in amusement. "That's not a wolf. It's a coyote, and the bird is a roadrunner. Those are really old cartoons. They were around even before I was born."

"Really? Wow. Did you have fun at your spa

thing? Grandma said you went to get pampered and stuff."

She didn't know what to say about her phony spa weekend. She certainly couldn't admit that she'd lied about where she'd been or how badly she was hurting over Zeke. "I'm just happy to be home with you now."

"I'm glad you're back, too. I'm getting kind of hungry, though."

"I'll fix you something. How does soup and crackers sound?"

"Good. But can I have one of those parfait cups with the whipped cream and strawberry goop, too?"

"You got it. Soup and goop coming right up."

She returned to the kitchen and prepared his food, running on nervous energy. Her mom hung around instead of going home. Was she waiting for Margot to calm down a bit?

After everything was ready, Margot brought Liam his tray. She'd given him two parfait cups and lots of crackers.

"It's chicken noodle," she said about the soup.

"Thanks." He smiled. "I love you."

"I love you, too." Such an easy kind of love, she thought. So different from the tortured love that she and Zeke were feeling. "I'll leave you alone now. But text me if you need anything else." She'd given him a kid's watch that allowed him to communicate with her. It even had a GPS so she could track him. He didn't always wear it, though. Sometimes he forgot. She walked over to the door. "Bye, sweetie."

"Bye." He spooned into his soup and returned his attention to the cartoon. Coyote was lighting a stick of dynamite that was about to explode in his face. Not exactly the best subject matter for a child, but Liam was old enough to know that it wasn't real.

She went into the living room, expecting her mom to leave now. Only she still wasn't ready to go. In fact, she plopped down on the sofa as if she meant to have a chat. She'd even reapplied her lipstick while Margot was gone. Her no-nonsense mother wasn't a glamorous lady, but she still took pride in her appearance.

"What's up?" Margot asked her.

"I was just thinking that for someone who just spent two and a half days at a resort, you don't seem very rested."

Because the spa hadn't been real, Margot thought, struggling with another bout of guilt. "Why would I seem rested? I came home to my son being sick."

"That's understandable. But you seemed out of sorts before I told you that Liam wasn't feeling well. I noticed it the moment you walked in the door."

Why was she still pretending? Margot asked herself. By now, there was no point in protecting her secret. "I'm sorry, but I've been lying to you. I was away on a trip with Zeke. We've been…"

"Dating?" her mom politely asked.

"No." She made the truth clear. "Just sleeping

together. I realize how blunt that sounds, but I can't think of another way to say it." She was beyond the lies now. "We had an affair before, too, for years after we split up."

"Oh, my. How did I miss all of that?"

"I was good at hiding it. We still love each other, but it's not going to work." She explained why their relationship was doomed.

Her mom's shoulders tensed. "Those are the same reasons you got divorced."

"And this time I don't even have a job. On top of everything else, *The Grown-up Years* was canceled. The producers had a beef with the network."

"Oh, honey. I'm so sorry. I remember how devastated you were when *The Kid Years* was canceled and now this show, too. You've been through so much already. It isn't fair."

"It's an awful feeling, believe me. But I'm going to tell my agent that I'm interested in other projects. Not sitcoms, though. I'd like to do films. I need a change in my life." Something to make her feel new and fresh.

"I'm glad you're picking yourself up by your bootstraps. But it's such a shame that you're hurting over Zeke. Why does he have to be so damned stubborn? Why can't he see the mistake he's making? He should be fighting for you, instead of letting it end all over again."

"He's never going to be able to handle my career. His issues with fame run too deep." When Margot's eyes flooded with tears, she turned away, not wanting her mom to see her cry.

Zeke wasn't going to alter his perspective. There was already too much anguish inside him, years of turmoil that couldn't be fixed.

Twelve

Zeke stood alone on a strip of white sand, gazing out at the water. He'd been in Samoa for nearly a week, and normally this place gave him peace. Only this time, it wasn't working.

His grandfather—or Tama as Zeke called him—managed a resort on the south coast of Upolu. Guests could lounge on the beach, swim, snorkel and charter fishing boats. There was a restaurant, bar and on-site gift shop. Yet none of those activities was able to ease Zeke's mind. Surfing didn't help, either, and he was just a ten-minute boat ride to some of the best breaks in the area.

He couldn't stop obsessing about Margot. She was

in his head, day and night, and the more he thought about her, the lonelier he felt.

Tama walked up beside him, and he turned to look at his grandfather. They were around the same height. Tama's hair was long and gray, and his skin was deeply weathered and heavily tattooed, the artwork on his body a show of pride. These days, he lived in a bungalow the resort provided, but when he was a boy, he'd grown up in a nearby village and lived in a traditional *fale*, a house with pebble floors, a thatched roof and no walls.

Tama had met Zeke's grandma here in Samoa. She'd come to the island with a group of friends, and she and Tama had fallen madly in love. Within no time, they got married and had a son named Joseph. In Samoan he was called Sefa. But he didn't stay on the island. Sefa was a restless guy, a charming daredevil who moved to the States, became a well-respected stuntman and married a famous Hollywood actress.

And then I came along, Zeke thought. The product of that fateful union. Soon after that, his dad died. His grandma had passed away during that era, too. Zeke had no recollection of either of them.

"How are you doing?" Tama asked.

Zeke shrugged. "The same as when I first got here."

The older man frowned. Typically, he was a bright and playful man. But he could be serious, too. "What do you want out of life? What's the most important thing to you?"

"Truthfully? I don't even know anymore."

"Then what was the most important thing to you when you first married Margot?"

"Just being with her and creating a life together. I imagined us having kids and doing whatever else families do." Zeke sank his feet into the sand. "But that was before everything went awry."

"Do you remember me teaching you about *Fa'a Samoa* when you were young and how important it is?"

"Of course. It's the Samoan way." Traditions that went back thousands of years. A complex cultural code designed to teach people how to conduct their lives and attain happiness.

"And what's at the heart of our ways?"

"Family. *Aiga*," Zeke added, using the Samoan word.

"Family is the heart of the Choctaw people, too. Your grandmother came from a tight-knit society, and she instilled her beliefs in your father. But he practiced the Samoan way, too. He had to learn to walk in both worlds. Sometimes he faltered, though, and struggled with his identity. That's one of the reasons he left and went to America. He was trying to find himself, but he found your movie star mother instead."

Zeke went silent for a second, trying to imagine it all. "What kind of relationship did my parents have?

I know they met on the set of one of her films and had a whirlwind romance. But I don't know much about their day-to-day life. My mom never talks about that part. I think it makes her too sad."

"She loved your father very much, and he loved her, too. Their relationship was good, strong and happy. They spent as much time together as they could. But after they got married, he began to worry about how famous she was becoming. Everyone wanted a piece of her, but he just wanted her to himself."

This was news to Zeke. "I had no idea that my dad struggled with my mom's career. How did he overcome it?"

"He wasn't willing to lose her over it, so he didn't even share his fears with her. He just became the husband she needed, without her ever knowing that those things had crossed his mind."

"I'm glad he was able to do that. For both their sakes. But I can't get a handle on my fears the way he did."

Tama shook his head. "You're the last person who should be afraid of having a famous wife. You protect celebrities. You support them and their families. You give them the best part of yourself. So why can't you give that to the woman you love, too?"

"Because I need my private life to be calm and quiet, not centered around her public persona. I realize that this is probably going to sound like psychobabble to you, but I already knew from the beginning that I never wanted a celebrity wife. That it would be too difficult for me."

"Yet you wed an actress."

"She wasn't acting when we got married. She'd already left the industry then." Zeke watched a boat bobbing in the water. "After Margot rebooted her career, I was so hurt and angry over what she did, I could barely see straight."

"Maybe you should talk to your father about this. He was a young man, like you, when he resolved his issues."

Zeke expelled the air in his lungs. His grandfather didn't believe in a separation between life and death. He conversed regularly with his deceased loved ones, treating them as if they were still alive. But Zeke had never quite gotten the hang of that. "I'm sorry, but I can't go to him with my problems, not the way I can with you."

"You most certainly can. Your father didn't die here, but he is buried here, and now this is where his spirit remains."

"Yes, but if I talk to him, is he going to respond? Is he going to tell me what to do? Or how to cope?"

"He might," Tama said. "But you'll never know if you don't try." The old man patted him on the shoulder, then turned to leave. "I have to go back to work. But there's nothing more I can say, anyway. Whatever happens now is up to you."

Zeke watched his grandfather go, feeling more alone and conflicted than ever. He dragged a hand through his hair, wondering if he should try to talk to his dad.

But how would he go about it?

He couldn't do it here. A group of tourists had just arrived. He could see them heading in his direction, traipsing along with their snorkeling gear.

Happy vacationers, he thought.

Other people were playing and having fun, and he was scouting the best location to converse with a man he'd never even met.

Should he find a secluded spot near the lagoon? Should he sit beneath a coconut tree? Or simply go back to his room?

Zeke chose the latter. He made his way to his bungalow and stood outside the door, staring at it, not having the slightest idea where to start.

Maybe he should give himself a bit more time. He couldn't force a conversation, not if he wasn't ready.

He decided to head over to the gift shop instead. He always brought trinkets home from the island, mostly for his mother and sister. But maybe this time he could buy something for Margot and Liam, too. He was still friends with Margot. A painful friendship, but one just the same.

The lady at the gift shop greeted Zeke with a smile. Her name was Lucy, and she'd been running the store for as long as Zeke could remember. She was a strong-boned woman with a broad face and sparkling eyes. She'd grown up in the same village as Tama and had a slew of grandkids.

She left Zeke alone to browse. He chose a kava bowl for Bailey, a coconut leaf fan for his mom, and a T-shirt with a tribal design for Liam. Finding something for Margot wasn't quite so easy. Nothing felt right. He lingered, looking at everything. Finally, he zeroed in on a little basket filled with painted stones. He sifted through them.

They had Samoan words and phrases on them, with English translations on the other side. He spotted *welcome, good day, please, yes, no* and *thank you*. Another grouping pertained to family: *father/ grandfather, mother/grandmother, brother/sister, aunt/uncle* and *cousin*. *Husband* and *wife* caught his eye, too, striking an emotional chord inside him.

Still, should he get them? They reminded him of the conversation hearts Margot had always favored for Valentine's Day. She never wanted chocolates. She preferred those silly hearts.

Zeke sorted through the stones again. There was even one that had *love* written on it.

Rather than overthink it, he brought them up to the counter, along with his other purchases. Lucy took his money, his *tala*, and placed everything in a bag and wished him well.

On his way back to his bungalow, Zeke decided to talk to his father, out loud, right then and there as he strolled along the sand.

"Hey, Dad, I'm sorry I never confided in you before. It's all so new to me, trying to figure out what to say." He continued walking and talking. "I used to be married, but maybe you already know that. Maybe Tama told you about my wedding years ago." He glanced at the bag in his hand. "Anyway, I just got my ex-wife a gift." He waited a beat before he added,. "I'm still in love with her, and I want to be with her, but I'm struggling with what she does for a living. She's an actress, like Mom. Tama said that you had a hard time with Mom's fame, but that you worked it out."

Zeke went on to explain his childhood and how chaotic it had been for him. He was still talking by the time he entered his bungalow.

He sat on the bed, removed the stones from the bag, tipped the basket they were in and dumped them out. "This is what I bought for Margot."

He didn't get a reaction from his father. He didn't hear any voices or notice any spiritual stirrings. But when he looked in the mirror across the room, he saw a troubled version of himself. A man who'd hurt the woman he loved.

Was that what his father wanted him to see? The message he was receiving? A message that had been there all along, Zeke thought.

He broke eye contact with himself and stared at the *husband* stone, ashamed of the kind of husband he'd been. Margot had deserved better, so much more from him.

He said to his dad, "You were a good husband to my mother. You did right by her, proving that you loved her, and she doesn't even know the sacrifice you made." Regret stabbed Zeke straight in the chest. "I wasn't like you. I failed my wife. She's my heart, my everything, and I walked away from her."

He picked up the *love* stone. "I want to be there for her now. I want to be the kind of man I should've been from the beginning. To prove that I love her, not just by saying it, but by my actions." He closed his hand around the stone. "But will she accept me? Will she trust that I can change?"

Zeke knew that he could change. He felt it in his blood, in his soul. He'd spent too many years worrying about how Margot's celebrity would affect him, instead of focusing on the love and commitment he'd pledged to her on their wedding day.

It was different now. He was prepared to do whatever it took to win her back, to stand by her side, no matter how famous she became.

Yet the possibility of her rejecting him scared him senseless. But after the way he'd wronged her, he feared the worst.

"Do you think she'll take me back?" he asked his dad, without expecting a response. Even Zeke couldn't foretell the future. In this case, only Margot had the answers.

On the day Zeke returned to LA, he decided to swing by his mother's house. He figured that his sudden urge to see his mom had something to do with his attempted communion with his dad. Nonetheless, he was going to make it a quick visit, a few minutes at best. He couldn't handle much more than that. He was overwhelmed with thoughts of Margot and when he should reach out to her. Tonight? To-morrow? He was anxious, but nervous, too.

He parked in the circular driveway and entered the mansion. He was greeted by a housekeeper, who told him that his mom was preparing for a small af-ternoon tea party. Apparently, his timing wasn't so great, but he ventured to the garden anyway.

He found her fussing over the table. She looked elegant, as always. Today she wore a ruffled top and a linen skirt, her hair swept into an updo.

"Zeke!" She smiled. "I thought you were still in Samoa."

"I came back early. I'm sorry I didn't call ahead. I just wanted to stop by and tell you that I had a good visit with Tama." And with his father, but he fig-ured that was a conversation for another time. He couldn't just spring that on his mom and then dart back out the door. "I also wanted to give you this." He handed her the coconut leaf fan.

"Thank you. It's beautiful." She placed it on the table next to a basket of flowers, making it part of the centerpiece. "But I think I should warn you that your sister is on her way over, and she's bring-ing June and Margot with her. That's who this tea party is for."

His pulse nearly jumped out of his skin. "Then I better go." It wasn't his intention to intrude. He hesitated for a second. "I guess it's safe to assume that you know about my bungled affair with Margot."

She nodded. "June called me. She was worried about her daughter. That's part of why I planned this tea, to try to help ease Margot's pain and have a women's chat."

"That's nice of you." He was glad his mom had Margot's best interest at heart. "I messed everything up, but I want to get back together with her. I want to support her hopes and dreams. I want to marry her again and be the husband I should've been the first time around. But this isn't the right time for me to talk to her."

"Oh, my dear son. Anytime is the right time to tell a woman how you feel."

"Then you wouldn't mind if I stayed?" By now, he couldn't bear to leave.

"Of course not." She put her hand on his cheek. "I have faith in you."

But would Margot have the same faith? "I hope she doesn't think we ambushed her."

"I'll explain that you just happened to come by. It's the truth, after all."

Within no time, Bailey, June and Margot arrived. But he only had eyes for Margot. She looked soft and sweet in a pale yellow dress fluttering around her ankles. As soon as she saw him, she stopped in her tracks, surprised by his presence.

His mom jumped right in, as promised. "Zeke just got back from his grandfather's and came over to bring me a gift. He didn't know I was having this tea."

"Then you're not staying?" Margot asked.

"I am, actually. But not for the tea. Now that I'm here, I was hoping we could talk. Maybe go for a walk in the maze." The location of their wedding, he thought. That seemed like a fitting place for him to lay his nervous heart on the line.

She agreed to accompany him, and they left the rose garden and headed into the maze. In addition to the hedges, it boasted thirty-nine fountains and hundreds of metal sculptures.

Margot glanced over at him, but he hardly knew where to start. She was being quiet, waiting for him to say whatever was on his mind. By the time they reached the first fountain, he was even more nervous. But he couldn't stall. He needed to speak.

He started off by saying, "I made so many stupid mistakes in the past and did so many hurtful things. I'm so sorry for all of that. Truly, I am. But I'm ready to give you what you need. I want to support your career and stand by your side."

She flinched, the water from the fountain shooting up behind her. "Since when?"

"Since I did some soul-searching in Samoa. My fear of having a celebrity wife ruined our marriage. It debilitated me when it should've given me strength and made me a better husband. I didn't rise to the challenge. I didn't believe in our love the way I should have." He explained further, going deeper, telling her the whole story, including the part that involved his dad. He even mentioned the gift he'd bought her and how the words on the stones factored into it.

She softly replied, "It's wonderful that you made a special connection with your father and that the gift you got me was part of it. But how can I be sure that if we get back together, you won't freak out again?"

"Because I'm stronger now." He led her to a bench, where they both sat. "I swear, I am."

"I don't know, Zeke. I mean, think about it, really think about it. What if I go into film and my career takes off beyond my wildest expectations? What if your worst fear comes true and I become as famous as your mom?"

"Then I'll increase your security. I'll become your personal bodyguard, not just your husband. I'll do whatever it takes to give us a semblance of normalcy without compromising our relationship."

She twisted her hands on her lap. "In theory, that's an amazing concept. But if it doesn't work, we'll be facing another breakup. I'm afraid of making a commitment to you and things ending up in shambles." I can't let that happen to Liam, either."

"The last thing I want is to make a mess out of either of your lives. I love you, and I love your son. I'd be honored to adopt him and become his father. But you have to believe in me, Margot. You have to trust me. I need your help to erase the past and start over."

"This is all I ever really wanted from you, but now it just seems so surreal. Like a dream that could shatter."

"I understand." He couldn't force her fears away. He'd just learned to tackle his own. "We can take it slow if that makes you feel better. We could start dating again and going to public places together. Then you could get a feel for what a new relationship between us would be like." If it was up to him, he would marry her tomorrow. Only it wasn't up to him.

"I appreciate everything you're saying and everything you're offering, but whether we go fast or slow, the end result could still be the same."

He put his hand on her knee, needing to touch her if only in some small way. "I'm willing to chance it."

Her breath rattled in her throat. "But I don't know if I am. I need more time to think about it."

"Then I'll give you as much time as you need." There was nothing more he could say to convince her to be with him. Nothing more he could do, except hope that she loved him enough to decide that he was worth the risk.

Margot returned to the rose garden alone. Zeke left without seeing Bailey and their moms again.

Back at the gathering, tea and scones had already been served. All three women anxiously gazed at Margot when she arrived.

"Where's Zeke?" Bailey asked, leaping up from her chair.

"He went home." Margot planted her feet on the flagstone patio, trying to stand strong but afraid she might fall over. "He's giving me time to think. To sort through my emotions."

"You didn't take my boy back?" Eva asked, speaking in a gentle tone about her son.

"No, I'm sorry. I didn't. I love him desperately, but my head is spinning." Her pulse was racing, too. Everything was moving at a dizzying pace. "Zeke says he's changed, but I'm afraid that the problems we faced in the past could arise again." She'd spent too many years going back and forth, loving him, losing him, having two affairs with him. "It's all so confusing."

"Maybe you should sit and try to relax," Bailey said. "Do you want some tea? I can pour it for you."

"Thank you." She took an empty chair and scooted closer to the table, accepting the cup her best friend handed her. In the silence that followed, she could feel everyone watching her. They were all seated now. After a few sips of the Earl Grey, she said, "Zeke wants to marry me again and adopt Liam. But how can I marry him, feeling the way I do?" She looked across the table at her mom. "I remember how shattered you were when Daddy left, how you cried when you didn't know I was listening."

Her mother sighed. "It's devastating to have the

person you love walk away from you. But your father never came back. He left for good."

"Zeke keeps coming back to me in some form or another. But all I can think about is the pain of another breakup. I mean, how can I be sure that he's actually changed?"

"You can't," her mom replied. "Sometimes you just have to believe what someone tells you. You have to trust them."

Eva nodded in agreement. It was obvious that both moms wanted Margot to give Zeke a chance. But she didn't know if that was possible.

Margot turned to his sister. "What do you think?"

"Me?" Bailey glanced up from the fragile teacup in her hand. "I just want you to be happy, no matter what you decide. I want Zeke to be happy, too. In a perfect world, you'd be together. But perfect worlds don't just happen. There's a lot of work involved, and in your case, it would mean letting go of the past." She reached for a scone and tore a piece of it off, dropping crumbs onto her plate. "I've never been in love or had a relationship like yours. But I've spent a portion of my life watching you and my brother trip and stumble."

"Only Zeke isn't stumbling anymore," Margot said. "He claims to have found his footing." The man she loved was offering her his heart in a way that he'd never offered it before, trying to give her everything she'd ever wanted. Yet she remained on shaky ground, still horribly afraid of getting hurt.

Thirteen

A week later, Margot woke up one morning in a state of distress, still fighting the future. But this much she knew: her fear of getting hurt was tied to abandonment issues, starting with her dad leaving and escalating with her divorce and losing Zeke. She'd wanted so badly for their marriage to work, for him to support her career the way she'd supported his, to live up to their wedding vows, to make compromises.

Margot pushed away her covers and climbed out of bed. She slept in pajamas when she was alone, not naked like when she was with Zeke.

She walked over to her dresser, where the Samoan stones were tucked away in a drawer. Zeke had left them with Bailey to give to her, along with a T-shirt for Liam. Bailey had dropped everything off yesterday, but Margot hadn't given Liam his gift yet. Mostly, she was still trying to deal with the way her gift made her feel.

Those pretty little stones reminded her of the rose quartz at the mountain house, and in that regard, they made her nervous. But everything pertaining to Zeke was causing her anxiety.

Desperate to clear her troubled mind, she went into the bathroom. She washed her face, brushed her teeth and banded her unruly hair into a ponytail. Still clad in her pjs, she wandered into the kitchen to pour herself a cup of coffee. She'd set the timer last night to have a pot ready this morning. It was Saturday, and she was going to spend the day with her son, but she hadn't decided what they were going to do yet.

She leaned against the counter and sipped her coffee. She'd already told Liam that her show had gotten canceled, and he'd taken the news surprisingly well. But she'd assured him they'd be okay until she found other work. Her finances weren't a problem. Luckily, she didn't have to take the first thing that came along.

At this point, Margot yearned to play different parts, not get typecast as the same wisecracking character she'd been playing since she was a child. It was a risk and might not happen easily, but she was willing to take her chances.

She frowned at her cup. She was willing to take a chance in her career, but not in her relationship with the man she loved?

"Hey, Mom."

She glanced up and saw Liam. He looked cutely disheveled, his pajamas rumpled, his cowlick-stricken hair matted and messy.

"Hi there." She smiled at him. "You're up early."

"I couldn't sleep."

"Me, neither." She'd barely slept all week. "How about some breakfast?"

"Okay, but can I make it?"

"Sure." She appreciated his sudden interest in cooking. "What do you want to fix?" No doubt she would have to help him.

"Just fruit and cereal."

That he could do on his own. "Hot or cold cereal?"

"I like the cold stuff better."

"Me, too. I'll have a bowl of whatever you're having."

He chose his favorite brand of puffed rice and went to work on the fruit, a mixture of strawberries, blueberries and bananas. He rinsed and peeled and diced. Margot was enjoying watching him.

He looked up and asked, "How come Zeke hasn't been around lately?"

She scrambled for an answer. "He was in Samoa, and he just returned last week. He got us some gifts from there. I'll give you yours after breakfast."

"Cool. Was he visiting his grandpa?"

"Yes." And now he wanted to create a family with Margot. Her heart ached from the thought of it. An ache that could be soothed, she reminded herself. All she had to do was reach out and accept Zeke's offer.

But was she ready to do that?

Liam dumped the fruit in a bowl and said, "Zeke told me that Bailey's dad adopted him after his first dad died. It's weird that his mom is so famous. Him and Bailey seem so normal, not like they used to live in a mansion or anything."

"Actually, their childhoods weren't very normal. Photographers followed their family around all the time."

"Do you think that'll ever happen to us?"

"I don't know. But if it does, Zeke will beef up our security." He'd offered to do a lot more than that. But she couldn't tell Liam the whole story.

He plucked a blueberry from the bowl and ate it. "Has your agent gotten you an audition yet?"

"No, but those things take time. I'm not expecting it to happen overnight."

"Maybe you could be in a superhero movie. That would be amazing. I could tell everyone that my mom fights crime. Unless you play a villain. But that would be okay, too." He cocked his head. "Are you going to miss being Fiona?"

She smiled at his use of her sitcom character name. "There will always be a fondness in my heart for her. But I want to prove that I can be someone other than Fiona." Just as Zeke wanted to prove that he could be a different version of himself. Only he wasn't acting or playing a character.

He was proposing the real deal.

Margot's heart clenched. She needed to believe him, to trust him, to shed her fears and take him back into her fold. If she was willing to take risks in her career, then shouldn't she be able to take a chance on the man she loved?

The man she'd always loved, she thought. It didn't get any deeper than that. She needed Zeke Mitchell, as much as he needed her. Living the rest of her life without him seemed impossible. Screw her abandonment issues. She wanted Zeke.

"Are you okay, Mom?"

She gazed expectantly at her child. He had a potential father waiting for him. Just as she had the husband of her dreams, waiting for her.

"I'm fine," she replied, a sense of warmth spiraling through her. No fear. Only love and trust and strength. "How would you like for us to hang out with Zeke today?"

He grinned. "That would be great."

"I'll text him to see if he's available." Knowing Zeke, he was checking his phone at regular intervals, hoping to hear from her. "We should all go somewhere and do something fun."

Excited, Liam wiggled where he stood. "How about the museum with the dinosaur bones?"

"You mean the Natural History Museum?"

"Yeah, that's the place. I was sick the day my class went there on a field trip. That was last year, before you adopted me. But I always wanted to see it."

"Then that's what we'll do." Her son could learn and explore, and she could be near Zeke and tell him how she felt.

Zeke stood at the entrance of the museum, waiting for Margot and Liam to arrive. Margot had texted him earlier and invited him to spend the afternoon with them. She'd also said that she had something important to tell him.

It had to be good news. She wouldn't have included him on an outing with Liam if it was something bad. But without knowing the details, Zeke was still anxious.

Was she accepting his offer to start dating, to go slowly, to see how things unfolded? Or was she ready for more?

For all he knew, this was a test of some sort, a meeting in a public place to see how he handled it.

No, he thought. She wouldn't test him in front of her son. Zeke just needed to relax and trust her judgment.

As soon as he saw her and Liam headed his way, his heart picked up speed. Liam waved and ran toward him. Margot walked at a regular pace, but the tender expression on her face said it all. Yeah, Zeke thought. This was good news, for sure.

Happy news. Loving news.

And at that moment, he knew exactly what she was trying to convey by inviting him to join her and Liam today.

She wanted them to be a family.

Suddenly everything seemed right in the world. Or in Zeke's world, anyway. The woman he loved wanted him in every way that mattered.

"Hi, Zeke!" Breathless, Liam stopped in front of him. He was wearing the T-shirt Zeke had gotten him in Samoa.

"Hey, buddy. It's good to see you. I'm glad the shirt fits."

"Thanks. I really like it. Did you know that they have dinosaurs here? And a huge collection of ocean biology stuff, too?"

Zeke smiled, imagining Liam as his son. His and Margot's. "It's nice that you're excited about being here."

"They have tons of stuff for kids to do. I wonder if we came here at night, if it would be like those *Night at the Museum* movies, where everything comes to life. Wouldn't that be weird?" Before Zeke could respond, Liam turned around to urge Margot on. "Hurry up, Mom! I want to go inside."

Zeke wanted her to hurry, too, just so he could be near her. She made her way over to him, and their gazes met and held. She reached for his hand, and he thought he might die. It was just a light touch, but it meant the world to him.

"Thank you for inviting me to join you," he said softly.

"Always," she replied.

Yes, he thought. *Always*. Her meaning was clear. Liam had no idea what was going on, though. He was still chomping at the bit for his museum adventure.

"Come on, you guys," he said.

"He's right," Zeke said to Margot. "We need to go in."

She nodded, and their first unofficial day as a couple began. But about thirty minutes later, while Liam played in one of the kid areas, Margot made it official.

"Have you already figured out what I wanted to talk to you about?" she asked Zeke.

"Yes," he replied. "But I need to hear you say it."

"Then listen when I say that I love you, and I want to spend the rest of my life with you. That you're worth the risk. That I trust you. That I believe in you." She moved closer to him. "I think you're going to make a wonderful husband and father."

He let out the breath he'd been holding. "I'll be a better husband than I was before, I promise you that. And I'm honored that you're going to let me be Liam's dad."

"I want to have more kids someday, too. But I'm going to focus on my career first."

"I'm good with that. I'll support you, Margot. I'll be the partner you need. I also think it would be better if I didn't travel as much as I used to. I can have someone else work with the out-of-town clients. There's plenty of jobs in LA for me, plenty of local clients to keep me in this area."

She smiled. "With your family."

"Yeah, with my family." God, he loved the sound of that. He glanced over at her son playing with the other children. "When are you going to tell Liam?"

"I think I should do it today. We can go back to my house later, and we can talk to him together."

"That sounds perfect to me."

"You can spend the night tonight, too, if you want. I'd love for you to sleep over. To start getting Liam used to having you around as much as possible."

"I'll be there. Tonight, and every night, until we figure out our living arrangements."

"I think we should buy a place together. We can find a location that's convenient for both of us. I know that Liam would love to be at the beach. But wherever we live, I want to keep him in the same school. It's a private school, so it won't be a problem."

"We'll make it work. But just so you're aware, there's a lady in the corner, snapping pictures of us." Zeke gave a slight tilt of his head. "She obviously recognizes you. But she's pretending to take pics of the exhibit behind us."

"I don't mind, do you?"

"Not at all. This is what I signed up for when I

asked you to marry me again." Zeke was prepared for having a celebrity wife, for accepting everything that came with it.

"She probably thinks you're my bodyguard. But with the way I'm looking at you, she might be wondering if there's something else going on between us. If she's a die-hard fan, she might even know that you're Eva Mitchell's son and that you're my ex."

"I'm not your ex anymore." He was her soon-to-be husband again. "I'd kiss you right now, but if Liam turns around and sees us, that wouldn't be fair to him. We need to talk to him first."

"I can't wait to tell him."

"Me, too." He wanted nothing more than to start their new life together, committing himself to her in every way.

Margot reclined next to Zeke in bed, too excited to sleep. Their talk with Liam had gone wonderfully. He was thrilled that Zeke was going to be part of their family. He'd actually jumped around the living room, shooting Zeke high fives.

"Liam's reaction sure made me feel good," Zeke said.

"Me, too. His energy is infectious." She turned onto her side to face her fiancé, the man she was going to marry all over again. "What kind of wedding do you think we should have this time?"

He leaned on his elbow, looking at her in the same awed way that she was looking at him. "If it was just you and me, I'd say to keep it simple, but I think that we should do something bigger and more festive for Liam. It would be nice for him to have everyone together."

"I agree." Wholeheartedly, she thought. Liam was a foster kid who'd never been part of a big, happy gathering that he could call his own. "Maybe we could do a beach ceremony. I can call an event planner and see what sort of oceanfront venues are available. I think a dusk wedding would be pretty. The sun setting over the water, flowers, seashells, a driftwood arch for us to stand under to say our vows." Her mind was filled with ideas. "But most importantly, I think Liam should walk me down the aisle." At their last wedding, they'd forgone that tradition. Back then Margot didn't want anyone giving her away or taking her father's role in the ceremony. But now she had a young son who belonged at her side. "I'd love to have that experience with him. As happy as I was at our first wedding, a part of me was still hurt and empty over my dad. But I'm learning to separate myself from that now."

"We've both grown and changed. It just took us a while to get there." He softly added, "Your dad might be gone, but I'm never going to leave you again."

"It's strange, but in some ways, we never really split up. How many divorced couples keep sleeping together?"

"We told ourselves it was just sex. But it was

more than that. We needed to stay close, so we used our affairs as a way to stay connected."

"We're definitely connected now."

"We most definitely are." He leaned forward to kiss her, slow and sweet.

They were already naked, so there were no clothes to shed, no barriers to get in the way. He ran his hands along her body, making her feel loved. But it wasn't just a feeling. It was a vow. She knew that he meant to keep his promise about never leaving her again. In her heart of hearts, she trusted him. Whatever obstacles they faced, she and Zeke would tackle them together.

He kissed her again, and she moaned her pleasure, eager for more. Not just sex, but the life they were going to live. When he entered her, she held him as close as she possibly could.

She breathed him in, luxuriating in how familiar he felt. He whispered in her ear, and she sighed. He'd just told her that he loved her in the Samoan language. He knew how to express it in Choctaw, too. Zeke wasn't fluent in either dialect, but he knew enough to get by. More than enough, she thought, when it came to whispering words of love.

She wrapped her legs around him, content in the weight of his body pressing down on hers. They'd left a night-light burning, and it flickered with a dusky glow, creating shadows on his handsome face. Yet as shadowy as he looked, there was nothing hidden, nothing to fear. He'd opened himself up to her, just as she'd done with him. They'd made an emotional pact to treat each other right.

He gazed down at her as if she was the most perfect woman on earth. And in some ways, she was. Perfect for him. Perfect for herself. She clasped hands with him, arching her body, moving in time to his rhythm, lost in the beauty of becoming one.

Epilogue

Life was good, Zeke thought. By now, he and Margot were searching for a house together. He was also back to work and staying with her while she went out on auditions. On their days off they hung out at his condo, where he continued Liam's bodyboarding lessons.

Today they were at his mom's, though, partying with family and friends to celebrate their engagement. Eva had insisted on hosting the gathering and making it a glamorous outdoor event, with catered food and floral arrangements floating in the pool.

It was an interesting mix of people. Most of Margot's friends were actors, and most of Zeke's were surfers or security specialists. Eva's crowd were Hollywood bigwigs.

His mom was in seventh heaven. She loved flaunting her celebrity. But someday Margot might surpass her. His fiancée was determined to revamp her career, and he was determined to help her. The complications from their past seemed so easy to overcome now.

He gazed across the patio and sent her a loving smile. She'd helped Liam get dressed up for this party, and the kid looked damned fine in his summer suit. He'd brought some school friends along, and they were oohing and aahing over the mansion. Zeke suspected that his mom was going to spoil Liam, treating him like her royal grandson. But that was okay with Zeke. Liam deserved to become a prince.

Zeke finished chatting with a colleague and approached Margot. She looked gorgeous in a long blue gown. She was also wearing her old engagement ring, the big shiny diamond he'd given her years ago. He'd offered to buy her a new one, but she wanted to wear the original one, saying that it had sentimental value. He agreed about how significant it was. He would always remember the first time he'd proposed and how excited he'd been, asking her to be his bride. He was excited to marry her all over again, too.

Once the cocktail hour ended and dinner was served, everyone sat down to eat. Zeke and Margot joined Eva, June and Bailey at the main table. Liam and his friends had their own special table.

Zeke reached for Margot's hand, and she leaned closer to him. Their wedding plans were in full swing. By now, they were opting for a fall wedding. Early fall, when the weather was still nice.

"This is a lovely party," she said to him. "And did you know that we're having banana fritters for dessert? Your mom got the recipe from your grandfather. But I was involved, too. I called your grandfather and told him how much Liam liked bananas, and he suggested *panikeke*."

"I love those, and I think Liam will, too. They always tasted like doughnuts to me. But you can put different toppings on them."

"That's what your grandpa said. I think it was sweet of your mom to design the dessert around Liam, but also with a Samoan flair."

He glanced over at the table where Liam and his buddies were behaving like perfect little gentleman. "I'd love to take Liam to Samoa. I'd like to take him to the Choctaw reservation, as well." Zeke's grandmother had been from the Mississippi Band of Choctaw.

"I'm sure he would enjoy that. You're going to give him a good life. We both are."

He looked over at Liam again, feeling like a dad already. He would be adopting the boy soon after the wedding.

As the dinner progressed, Zeke cut into his prime

rib and shifted his attention to his mom and Margot's. They were busy chatting with each other.

And then there was Bailey, he thought, sitting quietly across from him. She glanced up from her plate, and they exchanged a siblings' smile. She was helping Margot plan the wedding. She'd done that the first time, too. But weddings weren't always Bailey's strong suit.

Zeke said to her, "Remember when I told Mom and Dad that you wanted a bridal doll for your birthday? And then they gave you that wedding set you hated? The bride, the groom, the flower girl, the whole works?" He chuckled at the lunacy of it. "You were so mad at me for that."

She rolled her eyes. "It was the year I told you that I never wanted to get married."

"What the heck did you know? You were only seven."

"I was eight, and I'm still not sure if I ever want to prance down some aisle. Not like some people I know, doing it twice."

Zeke shrugged. "Yeah, well. I'd take notes if I were you. You'd be lucky to get a guy as awesome as me."

"Awesome? You?" Bailey gaped at Margot. "Can you shut him up, please? Like seriously, wipe that puffed-up expression off his face."

Margot laughed. "I could kiss him. But that might not be the way to keep him quiet."

"Yes, it is," Zeke replied. As much as he'd been

enjoying his silly banter with Bailey, he was far more interested in Margot's kiss. "It's the only thing that's going to shut me up."

"Are you sure?" she asked, teasing him.

"Absolutely."

"Oh, brother." Bailey groaned, and went back to her food.

Zeke didn't care about his meal anymore. All that mattered was Margot. He leaned into her, and when her lips touched his, everything went still. Even his heart. It was just a simple kiss. But it was filled with love and commitment, with every wondrous thing he and Margot meant to each other.

And he couldn't ask for anything better than that.

* * * * *

If you loved Zeke and Margot,
you won't want to miss
Bailey's story,
as the LA Women series
by Sheri WhiteFeather continues.

Coming soon
from Harlequin Desire!

COMING NEXT MONTH FROM

✦HARLEQUIN

DESIRE

#2809 TEXAS TOUGH
Texas Cattleman's Club: Heir Apparent • by Janice Maynard
World-traveling documentary filmmaker Abby Carmichael is only in Royal
for a short project, definitely not to fall for hometown rancher Carter Crane.
But opposites attract and the sparks between them ignite! Can they look
past their differences for something more than temporary?

#2810 ONE WEEK TO CLAIM IT ALL
Sambrano Studios • by Adriana Herrera
The illegitimate daughter of a telenovela mogul, Esmeralda Sambrano
is shocked to learn *she's* the successor to his empire, much to the
chagrin of her father's protégé, Rodrigo Almanzar. Tension soon turns to
passion, but will a common enemy ruin everything?

#2811 FAKE ENGAGEMENT, NASHVILLE STYLE
Dynasties: Beaumont Bay • by Jules Bennett
Tired of being Nashville's most eligible bachelor, Luke Sutherland needs
a fake date to the wedding of the year, and his ex lover,
Cassandra Taylor, needs a favor. But as they masquerade as a couple,
one hot kiss makes things all too real...

#2812 A NINE-MONTH TEMPTATION
Brooklyn Nights • by Joanne Rock
Sable Cordero's dream job as a celebrity stylist is upended after she
spends one sexy night with fashion CEO Roman Zayn. When he learns
Sable is pregnant, he promises to take care of his child, nothing more.
But neither anticipated the attraction still between them...

#2813 WHAT HAPPENS IN MIAMI...
Miami Famous • by Nadine Gonzalez
Actor Alessandro Cardenas isn't just attending Miami's hottest art event
for the parties. He's looking to find who forged his grandfather's famous
paintings. When he meets gallerist Angeline Louis, he can't resist at
least one night...but will that lead to betrayal?

#2814 CORNER OFFICE SECRETS
Men of Maddox Hill • by Shannon McKenna
Chief finance officer Vann Acosta is not one to mix business with
pleasure—until he meets stunning cybersecurity expert Sophie Valente.
Their chemistry is undeniable, but when she uncovers the truth, will
company secrets change everything?

HDCNM0621

*The illegitimate daughter of a telenovela mogul,
Esmeralda Sambrano-Peña is shocked to learn she's
the successor to his empire, much to the chagrin of her
father's protégé, Rodrigo Almanzar. Tension soon turns
to passion, but will a common enemy ruin everything?*

Read on for a sneak peek at
One Week to Claim It All
by Adriana Herrera.

"I want to kiss you, Esmeralda."

She shook her head at the statement, even as a frustrated little whine escaped her lips. Her arms were already circling around his neck. "If we're going to do this, just do it, Rodrigo."

Without hesitation he crushed his mouth into hers and the world fell away. This man could be harbor in any storm, always had been. His tongue stole into her mouth, and it was like not a single day had passed since they'd last done this.

She pressed herself to him as he peppered her neck with fluttering kisses. Somewhere in the back of her mind she knew this was the height of stupidity, that they were both being reckless. That if anyone found out about this, she would probably sink her chances of getting approved by the board. But it was so hard to think when he was whispering intoxicatingly delicious things in Spanish. *Preciosa, amada… Mia.*

It was madness for him to call her his, and what was worse, she reveled in it. She wanted it so desperately that her skin prickled, her body tightening and loosening in places under his skilled touch.

"I can't get enough of you. I never was able to." He sounded bewildered. Like he couldn't quite figure out how it was that he'd gotten there.

Welcome to the club.

Esmeralda knew they should stop. They were supposed to head to the party soon and she'd for sure have to refresh her makeup now that she'd decided to throw all her boundaries out the window. But instead of stopping, she threw her head back and let him make his way down her neck, his teeth grazing her skin as he tightened one hand on her butt and the other pulled down the strap of her dress.

"Can I kiss you here?" he asked as his breath feathered over her breasts.

"Yes." She was on an express bus to Bad Decision Central and she could not be bothered to stop.

Don't miss what happens next in…
One Week to Claim It All
by Adriana Herrera,
the first book in her new Sambrano Studios series!

Available soon wherever
Harlequin Desire books and ebooks are sold.

Harlequin.com

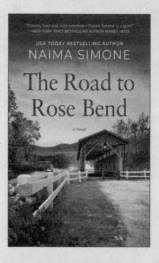